A Clearing in the Forest

A Clearing in the Forest

Gloria Whelan

G. P. Putnam's Sons · New York

Library of Congress Cataloging in Publication Data
Whelan, Gloria.
   A clearing in the forest.

   SUMMARY: An aging widow and a neighboring youth join forces to
wage battle against a powerful company that threatens to destroy the
northern Michigan woods where they live.
   [1. Conservation—Fiction.   2. Friendship—
Fiction]   I.   Title.
PZ7.W5718cl   [Fic]   78-3608
ISBN 0-399-20639-6

To Joe,
who looks through the same window

This is what I believe:
   That I am I.
   That my soul is a dark forest.
   That my known self will never be
more than a little clearing in the forest.
   That gods, strange gods, come forth
from the forest into the clearing of my
known self, and then go back.
   That I must have the courage to let
them come and go.

                              —D. H. Lawrence

1

Frances Crawford heard a gun go off. She stopped what she was doing and looked in the direction of the shot. "No Hunting" signs, all patiently handlettered and firmly underlined, were posted around the perimeter of her land. For fifty years she had fed the animals who shared her woods and river. She put out corn for the ruffed grouse, the ducks and raccoons, greens for rabbits and woodchucks, apples and a salt lick for the deer. She didn't coax the animals to her land only to have some fool hunter shoot them. Once or twice during hard times she had looked the other way when someone in town with a family and no job needed cheap meat; otherwise she enforced the signs, springing wrathfully out from behind trees like a wizened wood sprite, scaring hunters half to death.

Taking his cue from her, the large black and tan dog stopped for a moment and lifted his ears. Then, diverted by a chipmunk, he took off into some Juneberry bushes that bloomed along the riverbank. Moments later he emerged covered with pink petals, which he shook off like drops of water.

Frances went back to hunting wild mushrooms. Every year around the middle of May, people with bags and baskets slipped to their secret places in the woods to search for elusive morels that tasted, when cooked, like delicate perfume. There were as many formulas for finding the mushrooms as there were people seeking them: search the eastward facing slopes, around dead elm trees, in apple orchards abandoned by farmers gone to town. Frances's own formula never failed. She looked for the morels where the wild leek grew, following the leeks' rank odor through woods still boggy from the last of the melting snows. Showy white and pink trillium, yellow Dutchman's-breeches and adder's-tongues were blooming all around her, but the spring beauties which covered the woods only a day ago had disappeared, a sleight of hand that almost made her doubt what she had seen.

The run-off of spring rains and melting snow had cut into the riverbank, exposing new layers of sand and stone. It was like turning over a new page in a book. A small bit of shale caught her eye. Holding it in her hand, she could just make out a delicate tracery of fern leaves that had been etched into the rock millions of years ago.

The gun went off again, this time nearby. Ty Catchner's son, Wilson, strode out of the woods. In one hand the boy held the bleeding carcass of a rabbit and in the other a .22 rifle; a second rabbit hung from his belt, looking like a child's toy with all the stuffing out of it. Like father, like son, Frances thought. Ty always got his first deer the night before the season started.

The minute he saw Frances, Wilson started back into the woods like someone who had stumbled into the wrong room, the dog at his heels, hackles up, tail wagging in a terrible indecision that went straight to the heart of his character.

But Frances was ready for the boy: "Wilson Catchner, you get over here and tell me what you think you're doing shooting up this place or I'll set the dog on you!" Since the dog had made up his mind about Wilson and was now alternately licking the boy's hand and sniffing the dead rabbits, it was an idle threat.

If Wilson were not close enough to see the shingled white hair and the lined face with its faded tan the color of a fine old piece of mahogany furniture, he might have mistaken Frances Crawford for a boy of twelve wearing his father's clothes. A field jacket hung to her knees, its sleeves covering her hands. Her boots were so large she had to shuffle to keep them on. She must be at least eighty, Wilson decided. He remembered her husband, old Doc Crawford, who had taken care of him when he was sick. The doctor had brought him strange gifts: an empty turtle shell, the papery thin skin a snake had shed like an arm pulling out of a transparent sleeve, and once a bottle of tadpoles. "When the tadpoles have two legs you'll be out of bed; when they have four legs you'll be running around good as new," the doctor had said. And that was the way it had been.

The doctor had come to see him in a wheelchair, arriving in the back of an old pickup truck driven by Mrs. Crawford. It had been nearly five years since Dr. Crawford had died; from some sort of crippling disease, Wilson's parents had said.

The whole school had been let out to go to the funeral. Dr. Crawford had delivered most of the children and their mothers before them. Wilson suddenly wished he had been hunting on someone else's property. "I was on my way to the old Christmas tree farm and the rabbit ran in front of me," he said. "I guess I got carried away."

Frances thought Wilson must be about sixteen or seventeen now. He was a chunky boy with sun-bleached hair. Though it was early spring, he had the beginning of a tan. Nothing about his appearance suggested a sickly childhood. The boy had been born with a congenital heart defect, and after several years of nearly perishing with every cold he caught, her husband, Tom, had persuaded his family to take him downstate to the university hospital for heart surgery.

The surgery had been successful, but Frances never looked at the boy without the awe she felt toward someone who had been closer to death than she. No need to show him mercy on that account, though. "Where'd you get the other rabbit? I heard your rifle not five minutes ago. You must have been on my property. Can't you read those signs?" At the thought of the rabbit's tender flesh, something rather wicked occurred to her and she made her voice as firm as possible, "What are we going to do about this?"

Wilson reached down and scratched the dog's head. He wasn't making any suggestions.

"Those rabbits are off my land, correct? Suppose you give me one and keep the other." She imagined all the rabbits on her property cowering in their warrens at her words. Accepting part of his booty made a mockery of her signs. But the thought of a rabbit simmering away with some fresh morels was irresistible. The truth was it had been weeks since she had been able to afford meat.

"I'll skin it out for you, Mrs. Crawford." The boy had a broad smile on his face. Frances decided he was sharper than she had thought. No doubt she would see him during the deer season, but that might mean a haunch of venison to see her through the winter. She was disgusted with herself for being corrupted by the high price of meat. "Why aren't you in school today?" Frances decided to resume the offensive.

"School is a drag. I could stay away all week and not miss much. If I wasn't graduating next month, I'd probably drop out." He could hear his math teacher saying, "And now let's go over this just once more."

"You certainly have to have your diploma." Poaching rabbits was one thing; turning your back on mankind's civilizing force was another.

"I guess I'll work for my dad. I don't need a diploma for that. He doesn't have one."

The Catchners' front yard was strewn with cars and trucks. Anything with a motor that expired in the county was laid to rest on the Catchners' lawn. Nothing was thrown away. Anyone who wished to see the development of mechanization during the last thirty years could not do better than to stroll through the Catchners' yard.

When Wilson saw her frowning at him, he knew she was getting ready for a lecture. To avoid it he took a sudden interest in what she was holding in her hand. Like any child who has been seriously ill, Wilson was used to people watching over him and arranging his life; long ago he had learned how to distract them. "What kind of rock you got there?"

She handed him the fossil, and not abandoning his education altogether, advised him, "Those are carbonizations of fern leaves on there. Probably three hundred million years old, give or take a few thousand years."

"How do you know that?" Wilson was doubtful.

"I have a book that tells you all about fossils, Wilson."

He wouldn't mind reading a book like that. When he was sick for such a long time he had done a lot of reading. Every other week the librarian, Mrs. Walters, whose husband owned the bar on Dogtown Road, would stop by with an armful of books for him. His parents weren't very polite to her. They thought that all of those books weren't good for him, that too many words might clutter up his mind.

After he returned to school, he got out of the habit of reading books. It set you apart from the other kids, and he had had enough trouble after his surgery when his mother had insisted he be excused from gym and sports even though the doctor had said it wasn't necessary. At first he had thought he could make up for the fact that everyone regarded him as a weakling by showing them how smart he was, but it only made them dislike him more.

Not until he was fifteen did things begin to change. All the boys in his class were going hunting and he had asked his dad for a deer rifle. His mother had a fit. She said he'd catch his death of cold or get shot. She went around for three days not talking to either of them, but his dad bought him a gun all the same. When the time came, all his mother could do was make him wear long underwear and lug a thermos of hot soup.

He had hunted with two other boys and had been the only one to get his deer. His dad thought it was just beginner's luck, but it wasn't. As soon as he got the rifle, he had taken books and magazines on hunting out of the library. His dad would never believe you could learn anything practical from books, but that wasn't true. While his dad messed around with an engine, trying one thing and then another, he'd get a manual out of the library for the car they were working on. When he figured something out first, his dad was half proud of him, half sore as hell. Wilson had learned to keep his mouth shut, but he already knew more about diesels than his dad. Yet it was hard always keeping quiet about what you knew.

He said to Frances, "I've got some samples of cuttings from the oil wells, some from 7,000 feet down." His brother-in-law, who worked on the rigs had given them to him. The cuttings were brought up by a special drill bit. The core told the drillers just where they were. One of the cores he had was pure salt.

At the mention of the oil wells Frances frowned. She did not want to hear anything about the wells that had sprung up all over the county in the last two years. The very thought of them infuriated her. Oil wells belonged in Texas or Oklahoma, not up here in the woods of northern Michigan; certainly not a few threatening miles from her own property and the river. But she saw how the boy's closed face had grown animated, so she asked, "Do you know how the oil is trapped down in the ground?"

He didn't.

She bent over and picked up a porous rock to demonstrate how the oil migrated through the ground to rock that it could permeate. She showed him how water infiltrated the rock, too, and how the oil rose to the top of the water-soaked rock. She found some shale and told him how the oil gathered into pools under the shale, which the oil couldn't penetrate. Just as she was warming up to the subject, illustrating how the rock strata were shaped into a dome to hold the oil, a dizziness like a sudden push made her stumble and drop to the ground. The last thing she remembered was the startled look on Wilson's face.

Wilson tried to think what you were supposed to do when someone fainted. Before he could decide, Frances Crawford opened her eyes and began struggling to get up.

"Don't just stand there, boy," she said. "Give me a hand."

2

Wilson helped Frances up, amazed at how light she was. It was like holding an abandoned bird's nest in your hand. "Want me to walk you up to your cabin?" Wilson was embarrassed. If she passed out again, he would have to carry her. And she looked so old, brittle and dried up, he was almost afraid she would break into pieces.

But she started toward the cabin with no difficulty. "You bring the rabbit for me, will you, Wilson?" This was awkward, she thought. The old heart was having trouble pushing blood through her clogged arteries—not a good sign.

They walked along silently, following the river. Once Frances stopped and pointed. In the shadow of a log, a big trout lay suspended in water so clear it seemed not to be there at all. The trout's head was pointed upstream. He was waiting for the current to sweep an insect his way. It took Wilson a minute or two to see the fish. He decided there was nothing wrong with the old lady's eyes.

The Crawford cabin stood on a small rise overlooking the stream. To one side of it was a vegetable garden covered with a thick mulch of leaves and straw. A path had been worn into the sandy soil from the front door to a ramshackle landing that extended out over the riverbank. On either side of the landing was a bench fashioned from split logs. On the opposite bank there was a stand of birch, maple and poplar trees. Behind it was an enormous Norway pine.

"Listen to that river, Wilson," Frances said. "Even in the worst winter it keeps flowing. It's stronger than the ice."

Wilson was surprised that he had not heard the sound of the river until she mentioned it. He watched her stride up the path, her legs lifting in and out of her loose boots like two pistons. When they reached the cabin, Wilson saw that the front door was partially open; flies and bees were winging in and out like casual partygoers.

"Can't close the door," she said to him over her shoulder. "Have to take it off its hinges one of these days and plane it."

Wilson followed her into the cabin. While she dropped into the nearest overstuffed chair, causing a little explosion of dust to erupt from the cushions, he looked around the room. Even the town library didn't have as many books. But what a mess. Plants were everywhere: avocado saplings struggling up from coffee cans, African violets multiplying in styrofoam cups, and long tangles of ivy growing like snarled hair from blue milk of magnesia bottles. Had he asked, Frances would have told Wilson that even at the age of eighty she saw to it that there were still plenty of things that needed her. Furthermore, the green plants served as a leafy barrier between her and the snow drifts that seemed to lean heavier each year against the cabin.

Newspapers and magazines were piled up in corners, dust lay on the tables and fluffy balls of it wafted around the room from the breeze that blew in through the open door. On the floor was a large water stain from a leak in the roof. There were stuffed birds, piles of rocks, an old hornet's nest, small bleached white skulls, barrels of corn and sunflower seeds and rotting apples that smelled like cider. Snowshoes were lying on the dining room table and fishing rods were piled up on the davenport. Tucked under the chairs were old bones the dog had contributed to the decor. Wilson could hear the dog lapping water in the bathroom, probably from the toilet bowl.

Frances heard him, too, and it reminded her that she was thirsty. "You might bring me a glass of cold water, Wilson."

Wilson looked through the cluttered cupboards in the kitchen for a clean glass and had to settle for rinsing out a dirty one. The kitchen floor felt sticky under his shoes, and the dish towel he used to dry the glass was covered with stains. In a corner a dried-out leathery mouse lay in a trap.

When he handed her the glass and saw how her hand was shaking, he decided he'd better stay a little while. It was not a bad feeling, this looking after someone instead of always being looked after.

"Listen, if you've got some tools, I could fix that door so it would close." In deference to her age he spoke loudly.

"That would be fine, Wilson, but don't shout at me." She knew he was making up a ruse in order to stay and see if she were all right, and it pleased her. "Dr. Crawford's old tool box is right there under the table. I could keep the mice down if I could shut the door. I saw a tail sticking out of the toaster this morning."

Wilson's pounding and scraping cheered her. She had forgotten how pleasant it was to hear a man fix up a house. It was a lovely primeval sound that promised a snug cave with protection from lions and tigers—and mice. Wilson was a good boy. She would have to find some treat for him. From one of the kitchen shelves she took a dusty valentine box and tore off the cellophane. Hard to recall just how long it had been around. A patient might have given it to Tom, who hadn't cared for candy. Unfortunately the chocolates were rather gray, but some hard candies looked quite respectable. She plucked them out and put them in a little dish, first giving the dish a quick swipe with her skirt.

Wilson was putting the tools away when he noticed a large box filled with a number of perplexing things: straw, bits of string and yarn, unraveled sisal rope, dog hair combings and dust balls. It looked like something a witch might use to cast a spell. Before he could stop himself, he asked, "What's that mess?"

"That's my nesting box, Wilson. I'll put it outside in a few days and the birds will use the things in it to build their nests." She pushed the dish of candy toward him.

Wilson popped a lemon drop into his mouth. The flavor was very faint. He thought how different Mrs. Crawford's cabin was from his own home, where you could look around a room and see everything there was to see in just a few seconds; here, you could look and look. Beyond all the things were the books. He decided it was the kind of home he would have himself one day, if he could avoid marrying someone as tidy as his mother.

When she saw him staring at the books, Frances pulled one from the bottom of a pile, pushing aside the resulting avalanche. "Here's the book on fossils I was telling you about, Wilson."

Wilson held the book in his hands. The heft of it was intimidating.

"It's not a difficult book, Wilson. If you're interested in geology, you ought to read it." She was cross with herself. Who said anything about his being interested in geology? He would in all likelihood spend his life fooling around with cars in his dad's yard. She knew herself to be a great meddler. It was one of the reasons she saw little of people. The tendency on her part to give gratuitous advice disgusted her. After all, no one hated to receive advice more than she. She was horrified to hear her voice, presumptuous and carping, "Wilson, I want you to promise me you won't quit school; it's only another month. You might want to go to college someday."

Wilson was uneasy. No one in his family had ever gone to college. His older sister was the only one to graduate from high school.

Frances saw his hesitancy and said hastily, "Listen, Wilson, forget any advice I give you. I talk too much."

When he left, she walked down the road with him as far as her mailbox, wanting him to see that she was perfectly all right. The dog trotted ahead of them, sniffing out familiar landmarks. "I'll tell you how I find birds' nests, Wilson," she said.

"You take the same path each day, a trail like this one along the edge of the woods is best. You watch to see where the birds are flushed out as you pass. After you see a bird fly out at the same spot several times, you know just about where to look. Before the nesting season is over, I'll have found twenty or thirty nests just along this trail."

They came to a robin's nest in a young beech tree. Wilson saw that it was still in the process of being built. Like prudent contractors, the pair of birds had stockpiled strands of straw and strips of birch bark which they would work into their nest. Just before they came to the mailbox, she led him to a small fir tree. He couldn't see anything until she parted some branches and a brown bird shot out. "Song sparrow," she said. In the nest were two eggs of the palest green, spotted with brown and lavender. Wilson thought he had never seen anything more delicate. Beside them was a large white egg, freckled all over with dark brown spots. It was three times the size of the sparrow's eggs. Mrs. Crawford snatched it out of the nest and gave it to him.

"Cowbirds," she said distastefully. "Parasites. They lay their eggs in the nests of small birds that can't fight them off. When the eggs hatch out, the baby cowbird will be three times the size of the tiny sparrow fledglings and he'll get all of the food. The song sparrow fledglings will starve."

"Why don't the song sparrows destroy the egg?"

"They can't make the choices we can, Wilson."

Wilson held the egg in his hand. It was still warm. There was life in it. "How do you know you ought to choose the tree sparrow?"

When Frances walked back to the cabin, alone now, carrying the letters from the mailbox, the song sparrow had returned to its nest. Did it know the egg that would have killed its young had been removed? Probably not. Another example of her interfering. In nature the chain of casualties was long and complex and had a purpose. Wilson had asked the proper question: why the song sparrow? The boy would make a good scientist. With all her journals and notes, she was only an amateur.

Frances opened one of the letters. A local real estate firm had written to her again. They were always trying to get her to part with her land. River frontage was in demand:

> This is a premium time for selling your property . . . buyers in our office every day . . . future uncertain . . . under no obligation . . .

Someday they might get her land and turn it into a development with concrete roads and condominiums. But while she was still alive and kicking, no one was going to touch it.

When she opened the next letter, she saw how little her boast meant:

> Dear Mrs. Crawford:
> This is the third letter we have sent you regarding our wish to complete a seismological survey of your land to determine whether or not it would be worthwhile to drill for oil on your property.
> As you know, since you do not have the mineral rights, it is perfectly legal for us to go ahead with our investigation; however, we prefer to do so with your permission.
> I must also bring to your attention complaints by our crew that on a recent preliminary survey, some person or persons let the air out of their tires. The crew has also reported attacks by a vicious dog. We are anxious to do everything we can to foster good relationships in the community, and therefore in the interest of working out some solution which will prove satisfactory to all concerned, our representative, Mr. Clyde Looster, will be in touch with you in the near future . . .

When she got to the place where the robins were building their nest, she carefully shredded the two letters into long thin strips and hung them on a nearby branch in the event the robins ran out of birch bark.

3

Wilson pulled onto the sandy trail that wound through his front yard. As soon as he turned the motor off, the car became indistinguishable from the fifty or more cars strewn around him. Every once in a while the township supervisor would stop by on the pretext of wanting advice about a problem he was having with his car. After he had made the kind of jokes people make when their hearts aren't in them, he'd say to Wilson's dad, "Ty, it don't make any difference to me, but some folks along the road, and I'm not saying their names, are complaining about all the cars you got scattered around your lawn."

His dad would thin his lips into two straight lines, like he always did when he got angry, and say to just tell those nosey so-and-so's to mind their own business. "This is a free country and what I do with my yard is up to me and nobody else."

After some more talk the township supervisor would slink away and not return till the Catchners' neighbors got after him again.

Wilson noticed Lyle Barch had dropped off his motorcycle. Wilson had promised to fix the starter. He didn't much like Lyle, who was the kind of person who always looked right at you after he said something to be sure you thought it was clever or funny—and it seldom was. Wilson didn't like to be bullied into pretending to feel something he did not. Another thing he had against Lyle was the way he ran around with boys who were younger than he was so he could boss them. He'd buy beer for them and they'd race around on their motorcycles like a swarm of angry bees.

He pushed open the screen door and carefully wiped his feet. To make up for the disorder in the front yard, his mom kept the inside of the house immaculate. If you moved so much as an ashtray out of its place, she would call from someplace in the house, "Wilson, what are you up to?"

He found his parents where they were every afternoon before dinner, his mom at the stove and his dad at the kitchen table, newspaper spread out, reading out loud to her back. His dad didn't consider a newspaper properly read until he had made a pronouncement on each story.

"What they need down there in Washington," he was saying. . . . He looked at Wilson, "Well, here's the hunter come home. Got yourself a rabbit, eh?"

His mother smiled at him, "You must be a mind reader. I've had a taste lately for a rabbit."

Wilson thought how young his mother looked compared to Mrs. Crawford. And you never saw his mom in old clothes or even slacks, just neat housedresses that all looked alike. "I had two rabbits but I left one with Mrs. Crawford. I got them in her woods."

While Wilson's father did not encourage anyone to tell him what to do with his own property, he considered a little unobtrusive poaching on the property of others good sport. "Well, I suppose you got yourself caught and had to hand one over. I've heard the doc's widow is having a hard time making ends meet. That sickness of his went on for a long time and those last years he wasn't able to do much business. You'd think she'd sell that property of hers along the river. She'd get a good price for it and she could move into town. Anyhow, I guess we owe her. Doc never did charge much when he took care of you; not that you were worth much." His father gave Wilson a friendly wink to show he was fooling.

"What do things look like down there? I heard she's gettin' a little funny living all by herself," his mother asked, and then, noticing his book, "What's that you're holding?"

Wilson started. He had forgotten to hide the book before he came in the house. "Just something on geology Mrs. Crawford gave me to read." He carefully laid the rabbit down on some old newspapers and started for his room.

"Let's see it." His father held out his hand.

Wilson turned over the book. His mother walked over to the kitchen table and stood looking soberly over his father's shoulder as he turned the pages.

"Wilson, I don't want to see you with anymore books that talk about the earth being millions of years old. That goes against what we believe in this house and you know it." His dad slammed the book shut. "That's just nonsense. How does anyone know what happened that long ago? The devil could have put those fossils there just to mislead us. I want you to take that book back to Mrs. Crawford tomorrow."

"Dad, what if I was to go to college? I'd be seeing books like that all the time." Wilson saw his mistake as soon as the words were out of his mouth.

"That's just why you *aren't* going to college. What's the point getting a lot of education? You read all the time about young kids coming out of college and ending up waiting on tables. You can make all the money you want working for me."

His mother never liked to hear people arguing. "You get upstairs now," she said to Wilson, "and get yourself cleaned up. Dinner will be ready in half an hour and it's pot roast."

Once he had shut his door behind him, Wilson felt better. He thought he could probably get through anything if he could just know that at the end of it he would be all alone in his room or out in the woods by himself with a chance to think over what had happened.

He picked up a coffee can full of Petoskey stones and dumped them onto his bed. You could find them all over the northern part of the state. It was a rather nondescript rock which came in all sizes, brownish gray with a pattern of little hexagons that were anywhere from a quarter of an inch to two inches across. Each hexagon had a slightly pitted center. After you polished the rocks, the little centers of the hexagons stared out at you like a lot of shiny eyes. All the kids collected Petoskey stones. The stores in town had them made up into jewelry and sold them for high prices.

Wilson looked through Mrs. Crawford's book. There they were. The book said the stones were fragments from the ancient Devonian coral reefs that had existed 400 million years ago when a great salt sea had covered the whole state. Each one of the hexagons was a small animal; each shiny eye a mouth. He decided that when he returned Mrs. Crawford's book to her, he would take along his collection of rocks. He could see her sharp bright eyes looking at him, wanting to tell him—what?

4

The moment she heard the car approach, Frances Crawford escaped through the back door, stopping only long enough to pick up her berry basket. Peering out from behind a tree at the top of the bank, she saw the man knocking at her front door. He seemed to be acquainted with the dog; in fact he was giving the dog something to eat and the dog was fawning all over him in gratitude. Disgraceful! Frances turned away and headed into the woods, noting with distaste how a motorcycle had beaten down a path through one of the small stands of maidenhair fern.

When she came to the meadow, she found that the handsome flowers with ugly names were in bloom: ragwort, boneset, and viper's bugloss. She hunched down over what appeared to be a copse of diminutive cedar and pine trees, none of them more than ten inches high. They were *Lycopodi,* descendants of the ancient tree club mosses. Four hundred million years ago they were giant trees rising a hundred feet into the air. Unable to survive as large trees, they modestly reduced their size. And here they were.

A black flower beetle, glistening like a chip of coal, lumbered through a forest of slender green stems. Each stem supported a cluster of wild strawberries. Frances sat down and began to gather the berries. It was the only way to pick them. If you stood up and looked down, the tiny fruit disappeared beneath its leaves.

Her hands grew red; so did her mouth. Red stains covered her slacks and shoes as she inched her way from one patch to another. While she picked, she was in a green room with walls of bracken and a moss floor. The ceiling of maple and oak leaves produced a filtered light, dim in the early morning hours, and then, as the sun moved overhead, dazzling. Ants came to investigate the strawberry juice on her knees.

Around noon, certain the man would have tired of waiting, she started back to her cabin only to find that he had outwaited her. He sat peacefully looking out at the river from her lawn chair. Before she could turn back, the dog, who had been sleeping at the man's side, saw her and raced up the bank. There was nothing to do but go down and have it over with.

The man placed a long leg on either side of the sling chair and stood up. He had not been prepared for someone so old. With her wrinkled face and small trim body, Frances Crawford looked like the little dolls his grandmother had fashioned from shriveled apples. But he was only momentarily disconcerted. He knew he had a way with the ladies, never mind what their age.

"I guess you were hoping I'd get tired and go away," he said. "I'm Clyde Looster, the pen pal been sending you all the notes." A big smile followed each sentence. "I guess you know I'm with the Hutzel Seismological Survey Company." He handed her his card, which she took without wanting it. "We'd like your permission to do a little surveying of your land." He illustrated his speech by holding out the township map. An inked line ran between the river and her east-west boundary. He patiently shifted his weight a few times while she tried to study the map, but without her glasses it was fuzzy.

At last she looked away. "Certainly not," she said.

He decided to change his tactics. "Well, look at that, you've been picking berries. I don't believe I ever saw such little ones. Where I come from, it'd take a dozen of those to make one berry." Another smile.

She knew all about these people who worked for the oil companies. Since the discovery of oil in the area two years before, they were all over the town. They filled the two motels, and an overflow had settled into a mobile-home park, referred to as "oil city." Their trucks and cars had license plates from Texas and Louisiana and Oklahoma. Their wives could be seen in the supermarket, slim and friendly, calling out to one another across the aisles in girlish Texas drawls that sounded exotic in this northern state. The supermarket now carried collard and mustard greens, okra and black-eyed peas.

The children of the oil people were instantly identifiable by their good manners. Because it was so pleasant to be called "ma'am" and "sir" and have students stand up when you addressed them, the local schoolteachers forgave the children their frequent absences. When the yearning came to go back home for a visit, it was not unusual for a family to leave on a Thursday night, drive the thousand miles each way, and return early Tuesday morning. The exhausted children sat nodding sleepily at their desks, their faces sunburnt, fresh mosquito bites on their arms and legs.

The parents were strict with the children. Talking back could mean an instant reprimand, but no one else was encouraged to discipline them. A school-bus driver who had pushed one of them around for misbehaving had been taken off the oil-city run because the father of the child threatened him with a shotgun.

"My, you've got a beautiful place here." The man continued to grin waggishly at her. "I hope I didn't take a liberty by sitting on that chair there." The dog had settled down on the ground and was resting his chin companionably on the man's boot. The man reached down and thumped him.

"I don't know that you've got any right to be here at all." Frances was tired from being out all morning. Her knees ached and threatened to give out altogether. Her nose was running and she had nothing to wipe it with. When she tried to look up at the man's grinning face, the sun shone mercilessly into her eyes.

He moved a half turn so that he would face the sun. "Ma'am, it's a real pleasure to meet you. I suppose you know your husband's some kind of legend in town. They say Doc Crawford birthed over a thousand babies around here."

Tom would have taken the man in stride, had him in for a beer, found out where he came from, how many children he had, what church he attended and who he had supported in the last presidential election. He knew how to separate the enemy from the man without losing either of them. Once she let the man emerge, she lost the enemy, a dangerous risk in a war. "I suppose you've got a little speech to make to me," she said in a cold voice. "You go right ahead and then you can be on your way."

For an instant his smile went from high to low simmer. "I just wish we could be friends, Mrs. Crawford. I don't see but what we could do each other some good." He knew that she scraped by on almost nothing to keep hold of her property. His company made a point of seeing that the local banks got some of their business. Ralph Tondro, the manager at the Oclair Bank, had told him all about the Crawfords.

Dr. Crawford had been well liked in town, but he'd never made much money. During the depression years he was paid in cabbages and eggs, or if it were a big operation, a quarter of beef. When things got better and he might have earned more, he had come down with a crippling disease with a long name. Mrs. Crawford used to put him and his wheelchair in the back of their pickup and drive him around to make house calls. There he'd be, sitting in the back of the truck, waving to everybody.

The man smiled down at Mrs. Crawford. "What we want to do is make you a little gift, Mrs. Crawford, just for testing the property. And if we find something interesting, the company that will be drilling will be prepared to do more for you. Now we don't *have* to do anything. Since you don't own the mineral rights to your property, the oil company can come in anytime they want to, but we prefer to do things in a friendly way. We want you to be happy."

As Clyde Looster saw it, that was the crux of dealing with people. Find out what they wanted—often as not it was surprisingly little—and give it to them. Get them smiling. He prided himself on being able to make friends with anyone, never mind how mad they might be at the beginning. He had never had a man walk away from him without shaking his hand.

Frances decided further conversation with him would be interpreted as bargaining. "The only way you can make me happy is for your whole outfit to leave me alone. I do not want an oil well anywhere near this river."

Clyde Looster understood how she felt, but he had a job to do; if he didn't, someone else would. "You got to understand my company cares just as much about the river as you do," he told her. "The company is committed—" he disliked the word "committed," which he considered an affectation, but it had proved to be the right note on occasion "—committed to protecting the environment. We wouldn't dream of hurting this purty river."

"You weren't so committed when you drilled a well over at Sickle right in the middle of a bunch of sinkholes and didn't put down enough casing."

He flushed. Sickle had been front-page news for weeks around here. Gas had escaped and had come bubbling up like a witch's brew into a stream. There were explosions. The foundations of houses had collapsed and a major highway had buckled. The entire population of the town had been evacuated to protect them from poisoned water wells and foul odors. But it turned out that the company that had drilled had done nothing illegal. The state had no ruling about using casing at the time, and so the company had done what it wanted to, taking risky shortcuts.

"We wouldn't let a thing like that happen again, Ma'am. There are specifications now to protect you. Anyhow, this is just to test for oil. Chances are we won't find a thing."

She absolutely had to get inside to wipe her nose. "I don't want to have anything to do with your company, and that's final." The dog was lying on his back, ready to have the man scratch his belly. She gave the dog a kick and turned on her heel.

Once inside the cabin, she considered calling one of the real estate people. Let them come in and divide the riverbank into fifty-foot lots—the heck with the whole thing. She saw that she still had the man's card in her hand, and anxious to get rid of it, she opened a cupboard and was ready to toss in the card when five orange and black butterflies flew out, viceroys, *Limenitis archippus*. She remembered collecting the cocoons in the fall, cutting them off a willow. She had a tendency to act like a first-grader bringing things to school for the nature corner. After pitching the cocoons into the cupboard, she had forgotten all about them. Now the butterflies, newly hatched from the cocoons, dipped and fluttered around her like maddened maypole dancers.

One settled on her shoulder. She took it as a good omen and was beginning to feel better under this new and fragile protection when the dog, who had been watching a butterfly hover over his nose, snapped it up and swallowed it, dusty wings and all.

5

By early evening she was ending the day as she began it, picking berries. The Juneberry bushes by the edge of the river were heavy with a rich purple fruit that made a delicious preserve. It was her best seller. Flocks of black-masked cedar waxwings and female rose-breasted grosbeaks had been at the bushes, but they ate only the berries at the top, leaving the rest to her.

When it became too dark to see the berries, she decided to do a little fly fishing. Since the dizzy spell she'd had the day she met Wilson, she had given up wading the stream and had cleared a spot along the bank of overhanging branches so she could cast without getting her line tangled in the trees. As people played a smaller part in her life, the stream became more important to her. The first thing she heard in the morning and the last at night was its unobtrusive ripple.

She chose an artificial fly, as close in pattern as possible to the caddis flies twitching over the surface of the river. During the summer the larvae of the caddis lived on the bottom of the stream in cases fashioned out of tiny pebbles. You looked down in the water at what you thought was a pile of small stones, and it began to walk away.

Except for a band of red at the horizon, darkness was flowing from the woods into the sky. The trout, rising for the flies, made little plopping noises like fat raindrops falling on the water. From somewhere downstream she heard the primitive bag-piping of a loon. Although it was only fifty feet behind her, the lighted cabin seemed to be in another country.

She stood on the bank, soothed by the rhythm of casting her line and retrieving it. The ground fog rose over the banks and tumbled around her feet, soaking her shoes. The loon was silent. She was puzzling over the way the red glow was growing in the sky when she felt a sharp tug on her line. She was con-fused. The fly didn't seem to be in the water; it was somewhere in the air. The tension eased and the line went slack, but the next second it was yanked in another direction. The tugging became frantic. She heard desperate squeaking noises, hoarse and sharp at the same time.

Something flew at her. She had hooked a bat. It had mistaken her artificial fly for a real one. She wanted to drop the pole and run for the cabin, slamming the door behind her. She con-sidered cutting the line, but she couldn't let the bat fly off with a hook in its throat. She might remove the hook, but the thought of reaching into the small red mouth and past the nubbin tongue and the fine ridge of sharp teeth was unthinkable.

She got a good hold on her fish pole and walked slowly to the woodpile, exploring with her hand until she felt a small log. Slowly she began to reel in, feeling the tug of the hook in her own throat. Terrified, the bat arched back and forth in diminishing circles around her head. She could feel the flutter of its wing close to her face. She set the line and threw the pole on the ground. The bat flopped helplessly on its short tether. She brought the log down hard, missing the bat the first time, but the second time she felt the small body collapse.

Once inside the cabin she wondered why she was so shaken; she had made harder compromises in her day. She took out her kettles and jars and set to work with great energy. The kitchen became pleasantly warm. On the stove, the Juneberries, mixed with sugar, surged up into a translucent red whirlpool, their skins popping open to release a rich fragrance. She filled the jam jars, covered the tops with paraffin, and put on her special labels. Then, accompanied by a little cloud of companionable fruit flies, she tackled the dirty kettles, scrubbing hard at the red stains. When she had finished, she placed the jars next to those of the wild strawberry jam she had made earlier, setting two jars aside in the unlikely event that Wilson would stop by again. In the morning she would take the rest of the preserves into town, where the specialty-food market which catered to the tourists sold them for outrageous prices.

Before heading for the stairway and bed, she turned the television to the local news. On the screen were pictures of a roiling fire, the flames billowing out like scarves of orange silk blowing in the wind. The announcer spoke in an excited voice. An oil well had exploded in the next county, sending flames three hundred feet into the air.

"The heat is so intense," the announcer was saying, "it could burn a man's skin at a hundred feet." He introduced a man who had been flown up from Texas to put out the fire. The man's face flashed onto the screen. "I'm gonna cap that son-of-a-gun," the man said. "I'm gonna take a walk into hell. Don't anybody pray as much as I do."

The reporter was clearly impressed. "How will you keep from being burned?" he asked.

"You have to know how to treat a fire," the man said. "You have to handle it with tender loving care, like she was a new bride."

Frances walked over to the window. The red line on the horizon she had seen earlier had grown, and now the whole sky was flushed with a red glow that rose and fell as though the fire were breathing in and out. Although it was ten miles away, its eerie light had stained the river a pale coral. Frances thought of the man who had come earlier that day with his request to probe her land for oil. How long would she be able to hold him off?

6

Wilson watched the last cloud of smoke from the oil well fire dwindle to a wisp and then disappear altogether, leaving the summer sky a clear blue. The famous man from Texas had capped the well, but not before the fire had complicated Wilson's plans.

When school let out, he had started to work for his dad. The Thrangs' bulldozer had broken down, and Wilson's dad was glad to have his assistance. It had taken them nearly a week to get it going. Working under the hood of the big yellow machine, Wilson felt he had his head in the mouth of a dinosaur.

At the end of the week his dad had reached into his pocket, pulled out the wallet Wilson had given him for Christmas, extracted some bills, and handed them to Wilson, who was too embarrassed to do more than glance at the money in front of his father. Later in his room he counted out the bills, and it took him such a short time he knew he'd never be able to save enough to get to college by working for his dad. He was too proud to ask for more money, and he was pretty sure that even if he did, this was probably all his dad could afford.

Since his meeting with Mrs. Crawford, he hadn't been able

to get the idea of college out of his head. In his early years, after he had been so sick, something in the way people regarded him led him to believe he didn't have many options. Life itself was gift enough. Now he was no longer satisfied to let his life drift.

Twice he had gone to the library and looked at college catalogues, as someone hungering for travel looks longingly at pictures of distant places. All the details: the descriptions of the classes and the dorms, the diagrams of the campuses, the qualifications of the professors, even the history of the schools excited him.

But when he saw how much college would cost, he knew the only way to get that kind of money was to work on the oil rigs, as his brother-in-law did. When he learned from Ron that the oil companies were hiring, he had told his parents what he meant to do.

They had divided up their objections like a debating team. His dad argued against his going to college; his mother took on the risks involved for the men who drilled for oil.

"I don't want you taken in by any of those fool ideas professors hand out these days," his dad told him. "You'll come back with your hair in some kind of ponytail, spouting a lot of fool ideas. I didn't even finish high school and I'm doing fine."

His mother had dropped out of school to take care of her brothers and sisters when her own mother had been taken ill. As a result, she had difficulty reading. She counted on Wilson's dad to tell her what was in the newspapers, and sometimes she would ask Wilson to read a recipe to her on the pretense that she had mislaid her glasses. Wilson suspected that she would secretly be rather pleased if he were to go on to college, but not at the cost of working for the oil company. Two men from their town had been killed in accidents while working on the rigs.

But if she would have had any intention of siding with him, the pictures on TV last night of the burning oil well would have been the last straw. She had turned on Wilson. "Over my dead body will you get a job where everything could just blow right up in front of you!"

Wilson knew that beneath all his parents' words was the desire to keep him from leaving home. Ever since he had been sick, they never quite believed he could get along on his own. They had to have him where they could keep an eye on him.

Guiltily, Wilson admitted to himself that their need to watch him all the time was one of the reasons he wanted to get away from home. Some time or other he was going to have to live a life of his own, just like everyone else. What he would never admit to them was that the thought of working on the rigs scared the pants off him.

And yet here he was. After breakfast with his grim-faced, silent mother and his dad, who had pointedly ignored him, he had given up the idea of asking for the car, and was looking for a hitch into town so he could apply for a job with Ffossco Corporation.

He stood a little distance from his yard, with its jumble of wrecked automobiles. Any suggestion of the violence in which they had once been involved was softened by the hundreds of field daisies beginning to blossom around them, making the rusting hulks look like nothing more than another crop.

Wilson had just started to walk in the direction of town when Frances Crawford's old truck labored to the top of the hill. He could see her sitting stiffly upright, the dog, ears erect, on the seat beside her. A lethal rasping noise was coming from the motor. Wilson stuck out his thumb.

The truck lurched to a halt and stood shaking itself while Wilson hoisted himself up onto the front seat next to the dog. As he slammed the truck door shut, he could see his mother watching from the window.

"Well, Wilson, what brings you into town this morning?" Mrs. Crawford was sitting on an old bed pillow so she would be high enough to see the road. Each time the pickup jolted over a bump, a little shower of feathers exploded from a hole in the pillow. He was surprised to see she was wearing a dress and had slicked down her hair into a sort of bathing cap arrangement.

"I'm going to apply for a job on the rigs. I figure if I work for a year, I'll have enough money to go to college."

But Mrs. Crawford was not as pleased as he expected her to be. She sat in silence for several moments as they drove past weather-beaten log cabins, battered shacks, and basements connected to the world above ground by stairways that rose up like periscopes and ended abruptly in a door. The people who moved to the northern part of the state were exhausted or desperate after a narrow escape from the city and glad to crawl into any burrow.

Uncomfortable about Mrs. Crawford's silence, Wilson said, "Your truck sounds terrible. Sounds like a flywheel is busted."

"I'm just hoping the truck hangs on as long as I do, Wilson, but it's going to be touch and go. How much would a flywheel cost me?"

"If you take it into town to be fixed, plenty. But I think we've got an old Chevy truck behind the shed. I'll bring the part out and do it for you. I want to get in some fishing and I got something to show you." Wilson stuck his arm out the window and held on to the roof of the truck to steady himself. The dog had now worked his way onto Wilson's lap so that he could put his nose out the window. "You could use some new shocks, too, but I wouldn't be able to do that."

"I don't mind the jolts, Wilson, they keep me awake. What did you want to show me?"

"I was over at Billins' gravel pit. Found a *Bryozoa subretepora*." He pronounced the Latin correctly, catching her reaction out of the corner of his eyes. "I identified it in your book, but I got to give the book back to you before it gets wet."

"Wet?"

"I've got it hidden in one of the wrecks."

"Why hide it?"

"It's my folks. They were upset about the book. They don't want me to read books that say the world is older than five thousand years."

"If God could make the universe, surely he could make it as old as he wanted to. You must remember that the men who wrote the Bible weren't geologists. They were holy men and poets. I'm sorry if I got you into trouble, though. Do you want me to talk to your parents and explain the book was my doing?"

"That's all right. I can handle them. Right now they're more upset about my wanting to work on the oil rigs."

"Wilson, I'm glad you're thinking of going to college. It's just that I'm not too enthusiastic about the oil companies these days." She told him about Clyde Looster's visit. In the middle of the story she stopped the car abruptly and pointed to plastic streamers knotted on wooden stakes and around the branches of trees. The streamers marked the trails of the teams exploring for oil.

"You can't go into the woods or even down into the swamps," she said, "without running into those plastic red and yellow ribbons. Next thing you know they'll be declaring them the state flower. But I suppose I shouldn't complain, Wilson. After all, I'm burning gasoline right while we're talking, but I don't waste it like a lot of people do. Like that motorcycle gang, for example, that rides around my woods all day frightening off every bird and animal in sight."

Wilson knew Lyle Barch has been harassing Mrs. Crawford. He had heard Lyle call her an old witch and brag about how he had made her so angry by riding up and down her drive with his gang that she had run out of the cabin shaking a broom at them. "Just like a witch," Lyle had laughed. Wilson knew he should have stood up for Mrs. Crawford, but the truth was he felt a little embarrassed about being friends with her.

"Still, Wilson, if someone has to work on those rigs, it may as well be you. If it helps you go to school, at least some good will have come of the darn things."

They were approaching town. On either side of the highway were supplies of stockpiled pipe, and yards where heavy machinery and oil tankers were parked. The storage yards extended to the edge of the road without a tree or bush to hide their ugliness. Next month a refinery would start its operation. What had once been a quiet resort village was now a boom town.

Frances knew it meant jobs for a lot of townspeople who badly needed them. But, sighing deeply, she said, "If I wasn't so old, Wilson, I'd head into Canada as far as a road would take me—and maybe farther."

The modern brick and glass building that was Ffossco's new headquarters came into sight, and Wilson said, "Here's where I get out. I'll see you soon."

All his attention now was on getting up enough nerve to go through the two heavy glass doors in front of him. His brother-in-law, Ron, had let him hang around the oil rig he worked on so that when he applied for a job he could say he knew something about drilling procedures. Ron had even let him study a manual which the company had put out for the men on the rigs. Wilson had not been reassured by what he read. The work was hard and dangerous; in some ways he hoped he wouldn't get the job.

Once inside, Wilson was relieved to see Pam Lufton at the reception desk. He had been sure everyone inside the building would be a stranger, but Pam had been a class ahead of him at school and they had been to parties together. Having big brown eyes, straight black hair and high cheekbones, she had been voted the best-looking girl in her class. She was part Indian, and her mother had come to the school to demonstrate how to make boxes from birch bark and porcupine quills. Pam's mother had worn a deerskin dress, beaded moccasins and a headband with a feather. The rest of the time she worked as a dental hygienist for Dr. Groat and wore a white coat.

"Hi, Wilson, what can we do for you?" Pam's tone was off-hand, friendly.

"I want to see someone about working for Ffossco's."

"No sooner said than done." She pushed the button of the intercom on her desk, and twenty minutes later Wilson had a job.

7

Frances, feeling awkward in a skirt instead of her usual slacks, pulled up in front of the store. The last time she'd brought preserves to Elkins' Market, Elkins had smirked at the way she was dressed and made a point of introducing her to one of the resort people in a rather snide way, as if to say, "Look at this old bird, what a character!"

Well, she wasn't going to be the town eccentric. Today she had fixed her hair and put on a dress that looked quite respectable, even though it hung a little loosely on her. Her legs were no more than reeds these days, and she didn't seem to have a fanny anymore. Instead of the old leather fishing creel she liked to use because it was so roomy, she was carrying a purse, one that had been her mother's.

As Frances walked into his store, Elkins had enough sense not to look surprised at her appearance. Perhaps he realized that he had gone too far the week before. Nevertheless, so there would be no question as to who had the upper hand, Frances warned him that she would be asking more money for her blackberry jam in the fall. He replied meekly, "You're the boss, Mrs. Crawford," and insisted on carrying the boxes of preserves in from the truck.

On the way home she pulled into Eric Peterson's farm to pick up a couple of bushels of manure. Peterson hurried out, trying to signal her away, but she paid no attention. Years of trying to make a living from arid, stony soil had made Peterson frugal and reluctant to see anything carried off his place.

"Eric, what's new?"

"It's gittin' harder to make a living every year, Frances. I hope you ain't come for any manure, because there ain't none."

"What's that pile over there, Eric? It's nearly as big as your house."

"Well, I'm goin' to use every bit of that. I certainly can't afford to go and buy fertilizer." He looked nervously at the bushel baskets she was lifting off the truck. "I can't let you have six bushels, Frances. Only three, and that's a special favor."

"Fine, three is all I need, but I can't lift the baskets down from the truck if they're more than half-filled."

After some haggling, Frances settled on what she owed him. As she was about to leave, Peterson's wife, Mavis, hurried out with a paper plate of warm doughnuts. "Frances Crawford, you going without saying hello? I just finished a batch of these. Take some home with you."

Mavis's generous nature pained her stingy husband. She was a big, hard-working woman, but however messy the job she tackled, she always managed to look like she was dressed for a wedding, hoeing corn in high heels and feeding hogs in a hat with silk flowers. Today she was wearing iridescent taffeta.

"Did Eric tell you the news, Frances?" "They're going to drill for oil on our land."

"You have the mineral rights?"

"Oh, yes, Eric saw to that. He always drives a bargain."

"I hope the well's successful, Mavis," Frances said. "They've been after me for months, but I don't want to have anything to do with them. I have nightmares every time I think of a well next to the river. But, like most of the people around here, I don't have the mineral rights. If I did, I wouldn't put a well there for a million dollars."

When Frances got home, she changed gratefully into her old clothes, unloaded the manure, and spread some of it among the rows of squash and melon plants.

At the river, where she went to fill her watering can, she saw a brown branch floating upstream. Impossible! The branch began to undulate: a water snake. She sat down to watch it, arm and back muscles grateful for the rest. Her hair was damp with sweat and her shirt stuck to her back. She took off her shoes and socks and waded along the shallow edge of the stream toward a green island of watercress, hungry for its fresh peppery taste.

Little pebbles rolled along the bottom of the stream. You could tell how fast a river flowed by the size of the stones on the riverbed. If the current was rapid enough, it would sweep even the fair-sized stones along with it. She could feel the current's strength against the backs of her legs. It was no more than a nudge, but it warned her that the river was not always gentle. It could sweep you off your feet and carry you into its deep holes. It didn't do to close your eyes to the cruel things in nature.

She knew places in the woods where you could almost feel the presence of evil. No wonder people breathed such a sigh of relief when forests were hacked down and stumps yanked out of the ground to make a farm, or when the fields and copses of farmland were turned into orderly neighborhoods. It was not just a primitive fear of lurking beasts, but something more that frightened people. They wanted to visit the woods, but they wanted to walk through them on well marked trails, and at the end of the trail they expected clean rest rooms with flush toilets.

"Mrs. Crawford, what are you doing in wading at your age?" A tall young man stood on the bank, scratching the dog's head. He wore a sheriff's uniform. "Come on out here, I got something for you you're not going to like." He reached out to give her a hand onto the bank.

"You don't look more than twelve years old, David. They must be hard up if they have to take boys like you in the sheriff's office." She rubbed her feet dry with a handkerchief and put on her shoes. "If you're here to pester me about a license for the dog, you can just take him away. He isn't worth the three dollars."

"I'd like to see the man that could take that dog away from you. The county's got better things to do with my time than send me out to check on dog licenses. I've got some sort of a legal paper here. What have you been up to?"

She didn't seem to hear him. "Come on in the house and have a cup of coffee with me. I'm chilled right through from the water."

"You'll have to give me a rain check. I've got to see about a B & E report at one of the cottages down the river. Took a little booze and messed things up. Probably a couple looking for a place to make out. Woods are still too cold at night for lovebirds." He held out a long official-looking envelope.

"I don't see how you can do the oil people's dirty business for them."

"They got their rights like anybody else. There are some around here that would say they've brought a lot of business to the county."

"Tell me what the paper says. I haven't got my glasses. And don't bother with all the legal mumbo jumbo."

He opened up the paper and read it out to her, nervous as a schoolboy giving his first report to the class. He knew all about Mrs. Crawford's temper. "It sounds like its an injunction. The company that tests for oil wants to gain access to your property for the purposes of 'exploration.' I guess you don't want them here. I don't blame you. It's just about the only unspoiled spot left on the river. I'm sorry it was me that had to deliver this thing." He waited for the explosion, but Frances took the envelope from him without a word.

"The Greeks used to slay the messenger that brought bad news," she said. "I never did think that made much sense. I could give you a beer, David, instead of coffee."

"You twisted my arm." He followed her into the cabin, hurrying a little to keep up with her.

8

Young enough to believe that the exciting things in life happened at night, Wilson was pleased to be working the late shift. Tomorrow morning if his dad didn't get him up to help him work on a car, there would be the luxury of turning over in bed and going back to sleep. Afternoons he could hunt for rock specimens and fish down at Mrs. Crawford's or just hang around enjoying the way summer days stretched out even beyond your expectations.

The drive to the state forest where the well site was located took about twenty minutes. His father had reluctantly accepted his working on the rig and had even allowed him to use a car they had recently brought back to life. His mom was keeping a tight-lipped silence, and lately none of his favorite dishes had appeared on the table.

The shadowy treetops swept past the car like black clouds. Twice the headlights illuminated yellow eyes; the first time they belonged to a white cat, the second time to a fox carrying a small animal in his mouth. The fox had been in no hurry, standing at the side of the road and staring at the car, his prey hanging limply from his mouth, dead or paralyzed with fear.

It was a shock to turn from the dark road onto the well site, where a cold white glare from the fluorescent lights flooded the three-acre clearing, giving it the look of a gigantic operating room. In the center of the site stood the derrick, reaching up a hundred and forty feet, a row of red lights on its tower to alert low-flying planes. Two-thirds of the way up the derrick was a platform. Last week when he had visited the well site where Ron worked and had watched him climb up to a similar platform, it had given him a funny feeling—like a rug had been pulled out from under his feet. The racket coming from all sides was ear-splitting; he wondered if he would get used to it. Diesel engines rattled away. Gears meshed and brakes screeched as enormous trailers carrying lengths of casing pulled in and out of the rutted driveway.

Two house trailers had been set up on the edge of the location. The trailer where the geologist worked was marked "analytical." Outside its door was a little heap of tagged bags containing cuttings from the well. The cuttings were cores of soil and rock reamed out of the ground by a special drill and shipped by the geologist all the way to Texas. There they were examined by computers and a determination was made as to the likelihood of finding oil.

Wilson hoped that later on there would be a chance to talk to the geologist and find out what you had to do to get a job like his. Wilson was carrying some fossils in his pocket just in case the subject came up, though he didn't see how it would. Hell, the man would think he was flaky!

Wishing he hadn't worn his good boots, he waded through soft mud to a trailer marked "office" and knocked on the door. He was worried about the lie he'd told the company about substituting on Ron's rig. Looking around the location, he realized how unprepared he was. If they told him to do something, he would stand there like a dummy, not knowing which way to turn.

The trailer door was opened by a slim man with a blond beard and a weary expression. "You Catchner? Wipe your feet good and come on in."

Inside the trailer Wilson saw that the proper location for everything was designated by neatly labeled plastic strips of the kind you punched on a tape. There was a pegboard on the wall, hung with tools. A hammer rested beneath its label; pliers, screwdrivers—everything was in its place. Over the stove was a label that read "potholder" and another that said "measuring cup." Both were where they should be. He looked around to see labels on drawers and boxes, on the door into the toilet, next to the light switches. Stealing a look at the man who had seated himself behind a table, Wilson had a crazy notion he might see labels all over his face: "eyes," "nose," "ears."

"My name's Pete." The man yawned deeply, his whole face turning into mouth. "I got your papers here somewheres." He handled a folder, but didn't open it. "They say you had some experience? You don't look like you had much experience of any kind." He gave Wilson a gloomy smile.

"I helped my brother-in-law out some. He's with the rig over on Sandy Lake Road." Since the man didn't seem to care too much one way or the other, Wilson felt relieved to be edging nearer to the truth.

"I hear they went down 7,000 feet over there and got themselves a real stink hole. You can smell the sour gas a couple miles away. They're going to get plenty of heat from the people around them, have to burn it off, probably." The man put his head in his hands and seemed to fall asleep for a few seconds. He stretched and rubbed his eyes.

"Well, let's get down to business. I'm going to tell you in no uncertain terms we stick to the rules here. My crew has a good safety record and I want to keep it that way. This ain't no playground. Hard hats stay on when you're on the rig and I mean *all* the time. Another thing, if I see a cigarette out there, the guy whose smoking it gets run off on the spot. I got five more months in this God-forsaken country before I get transferred and I don't want nothing going wrong before I get away."

"Pete?" Wilson had been thinking about something since

the day he had watched Ron climb up the derrick and had experienced a funny feeling in his stomach. "I don't know if it makes any difference to you, but I worked a lot around diesels."

"How's that?"

"Well, my dad, he's got a lot of old cars and trucks and we do repairs, rebuild the cars and trucks . . . " He wanted to tell Pete what he could do, but he didn't want to sound like a smart-ass." I just like to work around engines," he finished off.

"Yeah? Are you giving me the straight stuff? How about welding?"

Wilson nodded.

"I guess we can try you out, but first off you go up to the platform where T. K.'s working on the pipe and tell him you're starting out and don't know nothing and he's to show you around up there. Then see the motor man, name's Ferrelli, and tell him you're a big engine man and for the time being you can run around there with an oil can. And remember to keep track of the tools. Anything that's missing comes out of my pocket."

Wilson understood the labels.

"Coffee break's in here, follow the guys in," Pete continued. "Coffee only, you hear? If I find so much as a drop of booze within a mile of this rig, the man who's got it gets his bottom kicked by me personally. Now get going." He pushed the plate of cookies toward Wilson to show him the speech was a formality, but Wilson was thinking of other things and missed the friendly gesture.

The mud sucked at Wilson's feet as he walked toward the derrick. A narrow ladder ran up along the scaffolding to the tower. The first few rungs didn't bother him because he was too busy watching the big yellow block that held the drill shaft. The block was at least twenty feet high. Everything there seemed outsized. Looking down, he thought he recognized Lyle Barch. He had heard Lyle was working on one of the rigs and was sorry it was this one.

Wilson's hands were getting sweaty and he was having

trouble getting his breath. Heights always made him queasy. The only way he could bring himself to continue up the ladder was to stare hard at the rung right in front of his eyes, study all the shades of gray and brown and black in the metal, really look at it as though it were a painting or something he had to memorize. If he looked up toward the top of the tower or down to the receding ground, he got panicky.

When he finally pulled himself onto the platform, he was horrified to see the floor was nothing more than a strip of metal grating. You could look down between the slats a hundred feet to the ground.

"Welcome to the 'Top of the Rig,' gourmet lunches and dinners, bar always open." T. K. reached into his back pocket, took out a bottle of Jack Daniels, tipped it, and swallowed. He offered it to Wilson, who hastily shook his head, looking over his shoulder as if Pete might be floating around in the air up there watching them.

"What can I do for you, buddy?" He shifted the last piece of pipe out of its slot and looked like he was getting ready to start down.

He was tall—six-feet-four or-five. Wilson felt like Jack climbing the beanstalk and meeting the giant. Would he leave him here alone? Wilson grabbed the railing and managed to answer the man. "Pete told me to report to you, then go right down and work with Ferrelli." The lighting up here was strange; the red glow from lights along the side of the derrick gave everything an unearthly look.

"Ferrelli? Hell, we could use a man with us. Well, since you're up here, I'll give you the five-dollar tour. Next time be sure you wear a safety belt. Heard the score on the baseball game?"

Wilson looked dumbly at him, too frightened to hear anything, but T. K. didn't seem to notice and went right on talking in a friendly way. "That crazy pitcher the Tigers got—the Bird—I'd give a lot to get down to Detroit and see him. Working this shift, I don't even get to see him on TV."

Shouting over the noise, T. K. started to explain what he

was doing. Wilson kept nodding, but he wasn't listening. He was so scared standing way up there on the platform that he wished he were dead.

Finally T. K. shut up. Thank heaven he was going down first, so there would be something between Wilson and the ground. But when Wilson tried to follow, he couldn't make himself put his foot on the first rung. Then he saw the space between himself and T. K. grow greater and fear of making the trip down by himself got him started. Once they reached the ground, T. K. said he'd see Wilson later and took off toward a pile of casing. Wilson stood there shaking, wiping sweaty palms on his jeans.

Lyle Barch approached Wilson. "How ya like it up there?" His smile was derisive. "Wait till you get up there on the block."

"What do you mean?"

"Well, when we got to get up there in a hurry, we just hang on to the block and ride it right up to the top of the tower, like an elevator."

An elevator without any floor or sides, Wilson thought gloomily. He could tell Lyle was enjoying the effect his words were having.

"Never expected to see you here," Lyle said. Didn't think you were the type."

What type did Lyle mean? All kinds of men worked on the rigs.

For a while Wilson had owned his own motorcyle, a battered job he had rebuilt from an abandoned wreck. Lyle had tried to talk him into joining up with his gang, but Wilson had refused. Since then, Lyle wouldn't have much to do with him. More than once Wilson had seen Lyle's name in the Oclair *Tribune* for things like "drunk and disorderly behavior" or "careless handling of a motor vehicle."

Wilson understood in part what bugged Lyle. Until the oil boom, jobs had been scarce. There was no industry. All you could do in summer was wash dishes in the restaurants—and even for those jobs there was plenty of competition. You watched the summer kids walk around with their tennis rackets or flash through town in fast cars. In winter even the movie theater closed down. All you could do was go into Oclair and watch the level creep up on the big snow gauge in the middle of town. There had been times when Wilson himself had done things he later regretted, just because he was so bored.

He decided that as long as they were working together, they might as well be friends. "Do we bring our own lunch or what?" he asked Lyle.

"You can if you want, or there's a truck comes by with sandwiches and pizza."

"I'll see you at lunchtime, then," Wilson said and walked toward the engine shed. After the climb up the rig, the mud oozing up around his boots was wonderfully reassuring.

Inside the shed, there was a pleasant smell of machine oil. On the wall a huge hand-lettered sign read: IN THE EVENT OF A BLOWOUT ALL ENGINES MUST BE SWITCHED OFF IMMEDIATELY.

These were the biggest engines Wilson had ever seen. But, even for such monsters, one of them was vibrating too much. He looked for a wrench and found one beneath a label that said "wrench." Pete must have been here.

When Ferrelli came in, he saw a boy hanging over the number one engine, tightening up a bolt on the bedplate, a smile on his face.

9

Frances Crawford counted seven men, a car and a truck. On the back of the truck was stenciled in large red letters the word EXPLOSIVES. The men scrambled out of the cars and, lugging their equipment, headed north through the woods along a cable line laid earlier in the week. Every one hundred feet they drilled three six-foot holes. The dynamite men came along behind them and placed charges in the holes. Then, using a shooting box, the men set off the explosives. By monitoring the sound waves from the explosions as they bounced off rock formations thousands of feet below ground, a computer could estimate whether or not there was a chance of finding oil there.

The little army advanced efficiently, not stopping to rest until its men came to the riverbank, where they had to decide the best way to cross. One man pointed toward a shallow spot in front of Frances's cabin, but the others shook their heads. Instead, they took off shoes and socks, rolled up pant legs, and waded across a somewhat deeper spot, holding their equipment out of the water. The stream's iciness surprised them and they laughed and shrieked like school children.

On the other side of the river, they stopped to dry off. A couple of the men knelt down to drink the clear water from the stream. Finally they picked up their gear and disappeared into the woods.

Frances had been at the window all morning. Now she knew how the early settlers who loved the woods must have felt when the landlookers and cruisers came through the country- side buying up whole forests for the lumbering companies to cut down. The dog, hackles up, ran back and forth, yelping nervously each time a charge went off. When the explosions were no longer audible, she left the window and hurried outside.

She expected some drastic change—bits of the earth's crust scattered over the ground, a fire, craters. However, apart from the trampled bracken and some bare spots about the size of a saucer where the charges had been exploded, there was nothing to see. Perversely, it was not what she wanted. She would have been pleased to find beer cans, trash, dead birds and animals, the earth ripped open, anything to justify the rage she felt over the assault on her land.

But nothing was there except a July day full of yellow flowers. Goldenrod was in bloom, as was the St.-John's-wort, with its butter-yellow petals. The mullein blossoms had begun their long climb. Cinquefoil trailed along the ground, and beside the stream was a stand of jewelweed where dragonflies came and went.

Frances walked along the river, telling herself nothing would come of the tests, confident the river would contrive some spell to throw the machines off. She saw men in Texas puzzling over the computer results, "Look here, look at what that tape does when we get near the river, certainly can't be any oil there. We'll have to try elsewhere."

Her fantasy was interrupted by a rustling on the ground: a meadow vole after last fall's acorns. She passed some sickly chokecherry trees, shrouded with deserted-tent worm webs. The milkweed growing along the trail gave off a cloying smell. She stopped to pick some blueberries which grew on the steep bank. A white-throated sparrow sang from the top of a nearby pine. As she stopped picking to listen, the dog trotted by and upset her berry basket.

Reaching out to save the basket, she let go of a sapling she was holding onto to keep her balance on the bank. A rock under her foot gave way and she slipped down the hill, her arms and legs scraping against sand and sharp twigs. She tried to catch hold of a branch, but she was moving too fast. When she finally came to rest at the bottom of the hill, the basket lay empty a few yards beyond her. The dog had taken off after a chipmunk.

She tried to sit up, moving with great care. Her arms and one leg seemed to be all right, but the other leg was twisted under her body. There was a sharp stab of pain when she tried to move it. She felt it carefully. There didn't seem to be any break. Possibly it was no more than a bad sprain. Even so, it would be difficult to get back to the cabin.

She heard the voices of men calling to one another. At first she felt relief at the possibility of help. Then it occurred to her it must be the team from the survey company returning to their truck. It was insupportable that they should find her sprawled here, helpless. But how to get away? On her hands and knees? They would overtake her. She decided to stay perfectly quiet. If they discovered her, she would pretend nothing was wrong. She retrieved her basket with a stick so they would think she was picking berries. As she tried to get into a more comfortable position, a searing spasm shot through her leg. It was all she remembered until she came to, cradled in the arms of the large man who had drilled the holes for the explosives.

"Are you all right?" He sounded nervous, like someone who has just had a strange baby thrust into his arms. "I felt your leg before I moved you and I don't believe there's anything broken, but you should see a doctor." The other men were gathered around her, peering down, worried looks on their faces.

She felt like a senile Snow White surrounded by outsized dwarfs. And the clumsy oaf had had the impertinence to feel her leg! "Just put me down," she told him. "I can manage the rest of the way myself."

"I don't think you ought to put any weight on that foot, ma'am. It looks pretty swollen." The man was frowning.

When she began to wriggle in his arms, he reluctantly lowered her. The other men moved back as though she might explode when she touched ground.

And she did. She yelped with pain. Two of the men made a sling with their arms and silently waited. Without a word she lowered herself into it and put a reluctant arm around each man to steady herself. The procession moved toward the cabin.

"How did you know where I lived?" she asked.

"They briefed us before we came out. This was volunteer duty, like cleaning out a machine-gun nest. They said you might take a potshot at us." The big man laughed; the others grinned.

She felt better. She might be helpless now, but she had made them think twice about tramping through her property. "I don't suppose you can control the results of your tests, what they say?" For that she would be happy to play the pathetic old lady and even whine a little.

"No ma'am," the man said apologetically. "We don't have nothing to do with the results. They go right into a computer and then we send them off to the company. We never see the results."

So much for that.

They were at the cabin. "Can we call the doctor for you? Or we could bring the truck over and take you right to the emergency room at the medical center."

The thought of riding into town in one of their trucks was odious. "Thank you just the same, but I don't have a phone. If you'll put me down in a chair, I'll be fine. I feel much better." And then, with a terrible effort, she added, "I'm glad you gentlemen came along. There's some lemonade in the icebox if you'd like some." But the men seemed anxious to be on their way. Did they imagine that she had booby-trapped the icebox, she wondered, or put rat poison in the lemonade?

She hobbled over to the window and watched them squeeze like Keystone Cops into the small car and the truck and take off. What angered her most was that having tramped that land for fifty years, winter and summer, she had believed there was nothing she did not know about it. Now they had come with their fancy paraphernalia, and the fickle land had immediately yielded secrets she would never learn.

10

While Frances made a grumbling recovery from her sprained ankle, Wilson brought groceries to her and took over the delivering of her preserves to Elkins' Market. Even after her ankle had healed, he found himself turning down the sandy, rutted trail that led to her cabin. His days were spent at Mrs. Crawford's and his nights on the rig. He was amazed he could pass so easily between two such different worlds.

Today Wilson and Frances were sitting at the kitchen table. Spread out in front of them were some fossils he had found in the gravel pit and a pile of her reference books. Holding the fossilized pieces of coral in their hands, they tried to imagine from the illustrations in the books what the land had looked like millions of years ago covered by a sea of salt, a sea crawling with undulating animals that looked like exotic flowers.

"We're drilling through salt right now," Wilson told Frances. "My wrists and ankles are raw from the brine they're bringing up." This tangible evidence of ancient seas had been a revelation to him. Suddenly he remembered something, and with a pleased look dug a small fossil from a pocket. It looked like a pair of wings turned to stone by an evil spell.

"*Microspirifer,*" Frances told him. "You don't usually find them around here. I don't think I have one myself."

He held the fossil out to her. "Do you want it for your collection?"

"No." She looked at him hard. "I thought you were going to do some fishing." She began piling up books. It was too much to become attached to someone new. She wouldn't have it. Hers was a time of life when you ought to begin to pull away from people. And until Wilson had come along, she had done just that. In India people her age slipped off into the countryside to live a solitary life. Those left behind had the wisdom and delicacy to let them go.

Wilson, not understanding why Frances seemed angry all of a sudden, was grateful to tug on Dr. Crawford's waders and head for the stream. But before he could climb into the river, she was coming toward him with a cottage-cheese carton full of worms.

"I found them in the compost pile," she said proudly.

Wilson couldn't help laughing at her. With her small tan face cocked to one side and her short white hair standing up like feathers, she looked as if she could have pulled the worms out of the ground herself.

He knew she meant the worms as a peace offering. She wanted to let him know she didn't mind his fishing for the trout with bait instead of artificial flies. When he had first started fishing there, she had told him how Dr. Crawford couldn't stand bait fishermen in the river; "plunkers" he called men who fished with worms. Anytime he saw one wading the stream, he would put on an old khaki army shirt and a tin badge from the dime store, get into his waders, and stomp into the river carrying a folding rule and a pad of paper. He'd give the man a big smile and introduce himself as someone from the conservation department who was assigned to measure the depth of the river.

Keeping a few feet in front of the infuriated fisherman, he'd plunge his yardstick here and there, giving special attention to the holes where there might be a big fish and generally muddying up the river and scaring away the trout for miles around.

Eventually the conservation department had designated a stretch of the stream for "artificial flies only." But evidently the men in the department had never fully appreciated the doctor's impersonation of them; when the signs had gone up, the Crawfords had discovered the "flies only" stretch had ended at the beginning of their property.

Wilson left the worms on the bank and eased himself into the water. The current tugged at his legs as he made his way slowly over the slippery rocks. He picked out a fly cleverly fashioned from feathers and horsehair into a small green grasshopper. He dressed the fly with grease, as Frances had taught him to do, so it would float in a natural way on top of the water. Finally he stripped off some line from his reel and snapped the line upstream. He knew Frances was watching approvingly from the bank.

The fly bobbed along a riffle and disappeared in a little whirlpool. He retrieved it, false cast a few times to dry off the fly, and sent it down the same waterslide. Even in midsummer he could feel the icy water through his waders.

He rounded a bend in the river and was out of sight of the cabin. The bank on either side was lined with tag alders and willow, and behind the shrubs were tall pines. Wilson felt he was wading through a green tunnel. A mink swam by to have a look at him, his sleek brown body making parabolas. Mink were fearless; this one circled around Wilson, staring him straight in the eye.

He was so fascinated with the mink he nearly forgot his line until he saw his fly sink beneath the water. He set his hook gently. In a minute a trout rose about fifteen feet from where he was standing. Wilson gave him a little line, watching him swim one way and then another trying to shake off the hook. Little by little he reeled in his line until the trout was close enough to scoop up with the landing net. The trout was good-sized, fifteen or sixteen inches, his side dappled with speckles of pinkish gold and purple.

By suppertime he was back with four trout. He cleaned the fish, and together he and Frances examined the contents of the trouts' stomachs to see what they were feeding on: grasshoppers mostly, and one had a partially devoured crayfish in his craw.

After a dinner of trout grilled with bacon strips over an outdoor fire, Wilson and Frances started off into the woods for a walk, leaving by the back door of the cabin since a rather testy colony of yellow jackets had taken over the front entrance and resented anyone coming near their home. Wilson had offered to remove the papery gray nest that hung down like a pendulous balloon from the eaves, but Frances wanted to see how large it would get.

Since Wilson was due at the rig in an hour, they headed for Deland, only a short distance from the cabin. On their way they passed hundreds of rotting stumps nearly hidden in the second growth of maple and oak. At the turn of the century Deland had been a lumber town, complete with churches, hotels, taverns and even a sawmill. Trains arrived night and day to carry out logs which had been floated down the river from·the lumber camps. One by one the huge white pine trees had been timbered. Some had reached up a hundred and fifty feet into the air. "Higher than a derrick," Frances told Wilson, pleased that nature had outdone man.

Now there was nothing where the town had been but a few old foundations grown over with brambles, and a lilac bush that still bloomed every spring. The site of the old town fascinated Wilson. He felt as though he could close his eyes and hear wagons rolling down the dirt streets and the rasp of the sawmill.

"It will be that way when the oil goes the way of the timber, Wilson," Frances said. "The men will pull out, taking their trailers with them, and not even a foundation will be left to mark where they lived. Chances are, down in oil city, some woman has already planted a lilac bush that will outlast us all."

By the time they walked back to the cabin, little puffs of ground fog like balls of cotton had begun to roll over the water. On the opposite bank, fireflies signaled one another.

The only sound was the deep overhead note of nighthawks plunging toward earth. Wilson watched as the birds stopped abruptly in mid-flight and then soared upward again as though some invisible barrier they could not penetrate lay between heaven and earth.

"*Chordeiles*," Frances said. "Greek for evening lyres." Wilson made no comment. Frances expected none. The better they knew each other, the oftener they lapsed into these silences. Once Wilson had confided to her that sometimes when he was with people he had nothing to say, but they still expected him to go on talking. If you didn't they thought you didn't like them or wished you were someplace else.

"I've felt that way, too, Wilson," she replied. "I didn't even know those voices existed until I married Dr. Crawford and moved up here from the city. For years he was the only doctor for miles around, and he was often gone all day and part of the evenings. Living here in the woods, I was lonely and then I began listening to everything around me. To what the woods had to say and to my own thoughts as well. I found out that everything in nature has something to say, Wilson, even if it doesn't make a sound. Never be afraid of silence."

But tonight the silence was broken. Just behind them they heard a loud noise, something between a snort and a hiss, followed by a rustling noise and the sound of hooves thudding away. "What was that?" Coming as it did out of the stillness of the woods, Wilson thought he had never heard anything as frightening.

"There's a big buck in there, Wilson. He's been around for years. Thinks he owns the woods—and maybe he does."

"I'd like to see him when the hunting season comes," Wilson said, excited now at the possibility of hunting the buck down.

Frances looked at him thoughtfully. "I don't know that I'd want to go after him, Wilson." She thought of an old Indian legend of an enormous buck that would appear to the tribe's most accomplished hunters, leading them so deep into the woods they were never seen again. But she didn't want to spoil Wilson's excitement. She kept the story to herself.

11

After being shut up in the cabin by a gloomy week of August thunderstorms with nothing to do but watch the bread go moldy and the milk sour, Frances Crawford was elated to be outside.

The rain had stopped, but everything was drenched; it was like walking under water. Ferns and grasses and trees swam by. The wild asters and goldenrod were awash. A crop of early-fall mushrooms had popped up through the moist earth. Yesterday's paper reported the death of two people who had eaten poisonous mushrooms, probably the very species whose orange and yellow lollipop colors she was admiring—amanita, the destroying angel.

Tracks on the rain-washed sand told her she was not the first to travel the road that morning. A row of evenly spaced tiny paw prints followed by a slender rippling line suggested a meadow vole had been out hunting seeds. She had seen a hawk circling nearby and was surprised the vole had risked the danger of venturing out of its runways in the grass. A rose-breasted grosbeak sang from a branch high in a maple tree, the sun illuminating its red throat and breast.

Two deer had walked along the road. One pair of heart-shaped tracks were large, the other small: a doe and a fawn. When the tracks reached a large puddle, the doe fastidiously avoided it while the tracks of the fawn sloshed right through. At a clump of Juneberry bushes the tracks made a circle. Several tall branches had been tugged or knocked to the ground so the deer could get to the berries at the top of the bushes.

The dog sniffed; his nostrils quivered. She saw two brown shapes spring up. The large shape took off in one direction, the smaller shape in the other. Although the deer moved quickly, the effect was one of slow motion because of the way their bodies rose up in the air and seemed suspended there for a moment. They rose and fell in graceful arcs. The dog started after the doe, then changed his mind and was after the fawn.

Frances screamed a command at the dog, threatening him with terrible things. At first her voice was harsh, authoritative, with only a thin edge of disbelief. Then it became shrill, hoarse, until she could hardly get words out. She ran after the dog, but her ankle had not healed completely and slowed her down. Ahead of her she saw the fawn's tail like a white flag; close behind it and straight up in the air was the dog's feathery tan brush. Finally there was no breath left for screaming at the dog.

A raw pain of exhaustion built in her throat. The tall grass was wet and her clothes were soaked. Her shoes were like wet cardboard. She tripped over a log and fell onto the drenched ground. As she tried to push herself up, her hand sank into a sodden patch of dead leaves. By holding on to a tree, she got back on her feet. There was nothing to see. The fawn and the dog were gone.

Stopping to rest every few minutes, she headed for the road. Her hair clung to her forehead in wet points that dripped down her nose and cheeks and mingled with her tears. On winter nights when the dog lay in front of the fireplace asleep, his legs moving as though he were running, little yelping sounds coming from his throat, what had he been dreaming?

When she reached the cabin, she sensed something behind

her and turned. The dog was there, his breast a bright red, like some exotic four-footed bird. At first she thought the blood was his, that in protecting the fawn, the doe had kicked the dog, slashing his chest with her sharp hoof. Frances started to run toward him. But, no, he was padding along briskly, his feet barely touching the ground, panting from the run, mouth open into a wide smile, tongue lolling out and dripping saliva. He stood before her, his tail wagging. It was not his blood.

She grabbed him roughly by the collar, tied him to a tree, and washed off the blood by pouring buckets of water over him. His outraged yelps pleased her. She took longer than necessary. Little puddles of reddish water lay on the ground. Just as she finished, Wilson, driving his father's truck, rounded the curve in the trail. The truck rose and plummeted in the deep ruts like a small boat on a stormy sea.

Wilson climbed out of the truck. From a distance it looked as if she were giving the dog a bath. Then he saw Frances's dirt- and tear-streaked face and the pools of red-tinted water around the dog's feet.

"The dog ran a deer. A fawn I think. We'll have to track it down, Wilson." Before they started off after the fawn, Frances went to the closet where Tom's hunting and fishing equipment were kept. Lately she had been thinking of giving it all to Wilson. He was becoming a competent fly fisherman and the gun he used for hunting was not as good as Tom's. She found the rifle, loaded it, and handed it to Wilson, avoiding his eye. They walked past the dog, who was straining at his rope in a frantic effort to go with them. Neither looked at him.

They followed his tracks in the sandy road to the point where he had left the woods. In the forest the trail was harder to find. There was often nothing more than a leaf tinged with red or a bracken stem broken in half. Sometimes they lost the trail, turning off the wrong way, and had to double back. Then Wilson saw a streak of blood like a scarlet ribbon along the ground and knew the fawn couldn't be far away. They found it lying on its side, blood oozing out of its torn throat. It's fearful eyes followed their movements.

Wilson had thought if the fawn were badly injured he would have no trouble killing it. It would not be the first deer he had shot. But in hunting he had fired in the excitement of the chase. The deer was just lying there, the whites of its eyes turned up, its belly heaving.

Frances saw Wilson's face and reached for the gun, but Wilson shook his head and fired. It took two shots to kill the fawn. With the first shot the deer made some little scrabbling motions with its legs as though it were trying to get up. The second bullet went into its head and the fawn twitched for a moment and then went limp. Wilson handed the gun to Frances.

"No," she said, "you keep the gun. I've been meaning to give it to you." She would be glad to get rid of it.

Later, when Wilson returned with a spade to dig a grave for the deer, he found himself thinking of what the fawn would miss. It had died before its life had even started. Frances had told him not to be sentimental, that nature was little more than a series of predators preying on one another. She had warned him against attributing to animals the same feelings he himself had. But something about the deer's death made him value his own life. As a child he had been close to death and he had lived.

It took Wilson nearly an hour to bury the deer. His clothes were still damp from the sodden woods. Deep in the forest there was no sun to dry him. Even with the strenuous digging, he found himself shivering with cold.

He was grateful to turn onto the open trail and feel the warm sun. His sadness over the fawn's death disappeared. Everything around him seemed important. He noticed how many shades of purple there were among the wildflowers that bloomed this time of year, the asters and vervain and knap-weed. He found a translucent green stone, still wet from the rain. It looked like a small piece of deep water that had solidi-fied. He slipped it into his pocket, not caring that when it dried it would look like an ordinary stone. He would remem-ber what it had looked like now. A turtle was crossing the trail. Wilson stopped to admire the intricate red and black design on the margins of its shell. When he finally reached the cabin the dog, free of his rope, ran to meet him. Without thinking, Wilson reached down and ruffled the dog's fur.

12

Because the night crew was short of drillers, Pete had taken Wilson off the engines. Nearly every night now he had to steel himself to scramble up the ladder to the platform where he wrestled the length of pipe in or out of the slots where they rested while a new bit was attached or the well logged.

For a while Wilson had considered quitting rather than face another night on the platform, but Frances had encouraged him to stay on. "Surely you haven't saved enough yet to see you through school, Wilson?"

In a way he would have been sorry to leave the other men on the rig. After weeks of working together they had grown close and were proud of how quickly they could draw out the thousands of feet of pipeline or send it back down. He liked spending time with men like T. K. Dorp, who always seemed to have some wild story to tell.

T. K. got away with a lot because he was so experienced. He had been everywhere: up on the North Slope of Alaska and in the Middle East. He had taken a dislike to Lyle Barch, who was never fast enough to suit him. When he wasn't harassing Lyle, he was bickering with Pete, the tool-pusher.

Tonight things were going smoothly. They had made their connections in record time, and the four of them, Pete, Lyle, T. K. and Wilson, were sitting together eating pizza just delivered by the sandwich van.

The August sun had beaten down all day on the metal roof of the doghouse at the base of the derrick, where the tools and records were kept. Even though it was one o'clock in the morning, it was still stifling in there, and they were happy to be sitting outside in the cool night. The glare of the fluorescent lights made the location as bright as day, but beyond the lights the dark forest encircled them. Wilson wondered if raccoons and skunks and other nocturnal animals came to the edge of the clearing to watch them. Several times, just before daybreak, when they were up on the platform, they had seen a large buck wander down the trail that led to the location. It reminded Wilson of the old buck on Frances's land, the one he meant to go after when the deer season opened.

T. K. said, "Where we headed for after we finish this job up?"

Pete said, "I hear we're going to be drilling over near the Oclair River."

Wilson asked, "Where?"

Pete did not notice the alarm in Wilson's voice. "I heard there's some little old lady got some property along the river. Guess she's not going to be too happy about our drilling there."

Lyle was watching Wilson. He knew whose property Pete was talking about and asked, "Don't you know old lady Crawford?" He was enjoying Wilson's discomfort. Lyle resented the fact that Mrs. Crawford chased him off her property while she allowed Wilson to fish there.

Pete and T. K. looked at Wilson. "I been fishing down there a couple of times," he said in what he hoped was an offhand way. If they thought he was friendly with Mrs. Crawford, they might not tell him what information they had about the well.

Pete said, "Well, once she hears we're drilling over there, you aren't going to be welcome on her property. "Hey, Barch, where you going?"

Lyle had started off across the location toward his car. "Be back in a couple of minutes," he called over a shoulder.

T. K. spat a jet of tobacco juice. "Laziest guy I ever worked with. Don't know why you keep him on."

Lyle was taking a gun from his car. They watched him disappear into the woods in the direction of the trail, carrying the gun and a flashlight. They could follow his progress through the darkness by its beam.

Wilson took advantage of Lyle's absence to get more information about where on Frances's property they planned to locate the well.

Pete was in the midst of explaining when suddenly he jumped up. "I believe that son-of-a-gun is shining deer! Trying to attract that buck to the light. Doesn't he know he could get slapped in jail for having a deer rifle in his possession out of season?"

"He's lazy, but he's not dumb," T. K. said. "That's a shotgun. Anyone catch him, he'll say he was after raccoon."

"But using a shotgun on a deer?" Wilson was disgusted. "Half the time you just injure the deer and it gets away and bleeds to death."

"That's right, son, but Lyle isn't thinking about the deer, he's thinking about number one."

They sat watching the light move through the woods. With Lyle's figure invisible among the trees, the light seemed to have a life of its own. Finally the light moved back toward the location. If the buck had been out there, he had been too smart to expose himself.

Pete and T. K. exchanged glances and then winked at Wilson. As Lyle walked toward them, Pete said, "There's so much sand and mud around this doghouse someone's going to slip and break his fool head. Wilson, you get the hose out and clean up some of this swill."

The mud they used to lubricate the drill and keep any gas from escaping through the deepening hole was slick and slippery. Every so often they dragged out a big hose and cleaned off the metal steps and floor. On an especially hot day they'd turn the hose on each other to cool off, but you had to be careful, as it carried a great force.

Wilson held the nozzle firmly and called to T. K. to turn on the water. The nozzle was pointed away from Lyle, who was just starting up the stairway. When Wilson felt the hose stiffen with the full force of the water, he suddenly turned it on Lyle, who tripped over the bottom stair and fell back onto the ground, fuming and sputtering. His clothes were drenched and water ran in little rivulets down his angry face.

T. K. walked over and looked down at Lyle. "Hell's fire, Lyle, what are you doing down there?" he shouted. "We're already ten minutes behind schedule."

13

Abruptly, before Frances was prepared for it, autumn arrived. In the morning she was out under a hot sun picking tomatoes, warm and solid in her hand. By late afternoon the day turned from summer to fall. The sky was still intensely blue, but large swatches of white cloud rolled in ahead of a chilling northwest wind. Bright sun and deep shade followed one another. A goldfinch rode a swaying mullein stem, picking out seeds where only a few weeks before there were yellow blossoms.

After a week of rain the blackberries were plump with purple juice. They only had to be touched and they plopped softly into her basket. She saw that something had been pecking at the berries and solved the mystery when she came upon a buff-colored feather, dappled with brown. She stuck it in her hatband. A ruffed grouse was sharing her territory.

While she picked, two motorcyclists gunned down the trail not more than fifteen feet from where she was standing. Had they seen her? She disliked their obtrusiveness. In the woods you ought to behave like well-mannered guests who find themselves momentarily in crowded quarters. You slipped by one another, politely making room, lowering your voice, adjusting your schedule for the convenience of others. A thousand creatures might make their home in one square foot of ground, but they managed to go their separate ways. Even the small murders that constantly went on in nature were carried out with discretion; for all the carnage, you never heard cries of fright or the sound of jaws working.

After she had stripped the bushes that grew like a hedge along the trail, she moved deeper into the woods where the brambles were tangled into thorny arches that reached well above her head. They caught at her clothes and hair and left long red welts on her hands. Overhead clouds obscured the sun. For a minute, in the dark woods, she felt something close to panic and turned to be sure the dog was close by.

The clouds rolled away from the sun. She began to pick again. She set a limit for herself. She would stop picking in half an hour—an hour. But she picked on, compulsively. The bracken had turned to brown; its fronds constricted into shriveled.hands. This morning she was awakened by acorns pelting the roof. With all the signs of fall around her, each berry was summer in her hand.

Finally she turned toward the cabin, the dog and darkness at her heels. Lights were shining in the cabin windows and wood smoke rose fragrant from the chimney. She saw Catchner's car parked on the road and was about to call out to Wilson when the two motorcyclists came racing down the trail, shooting past her. In a moment they were back, making a wide circle around her. The dog watched the bikes, hackles up, his tail straight out, teeth bared. A low growl was growing in his throat.

Frances tried to see who the cyclists were. It bothered her that in the growing darkness she could not recognize their faces. In helmets and goggles, they looked otherworldly and menacing. She shouted at them, but the sound of her voice was drowned out by the rasp of their engines. One of the riders threw an empty beer can at the dog.

They made a second circle around her. This time they were much closer and she could see their grinning mouths. The most frightening thing of all was that they should enjoy what they were doing.

The next circle was no more than a few yards from her. Sand and gravel flew up from their wheels. A small stone ricocheted against her leg, making her cry out with pain. She dropped her basket and tried to call the dog to her. He was running back and forth, inches from the motorcycles, barking furiously. She thought of how wolves would cut off an old caribou and circle it before they moved in for the kill. The black jackets and black helmets of the cyclists blended into the darkness; only the lower part of their white faces was visible. Their disembodied grins swirled around her. "Dear Lord," she prayed, "don't let Wilson come out here." What could he possibly do against two of them?

The moment he had heard the motorcycles Wilson had turned off the cabin lights and rushed to the window. Even in the darkness it took him only a second to recognize Lyle's motorcycle. The second bike must belong to Steve Brathen. They had probably followed his car to Mrs. Crawford's with some idea of getting back at him for the hosing down he had given Lyle the night before. Wilson was sure Lyle wouldn't go away until he went out. But fear kept him at the window.

The motorcyclists turned on their headlights. As their circles grew smaller and smaller, Wilson could see Frances standing huddled in her old army jacket, the basket of spilled berries at her feet. Suddenly the dog lunged out at one of the cycles and the cycle swerved toward the dog, sending him flying. The dog yelped and Wilson ran outside.

Lyle turned his motorcycle toward Wilson and ground the cycle to a screeching halt inches from him. Wilson lunged at Lyle. He was past caring what hapepned to himself. The two of them fell onto the roadway. Lyle's helmet flew off. Wilson felt a blow that seemed to flatten his nose. There was a sharp pain in his head and he felt something warm and wet trickle over his mouth and chin. He tried to wrench Lyle over onto his back, his anger giving him a strength he was almost afraid to use. In seconds Lyle lay pinned to the ground, but Steve had turned off his engine and was moving across the driveway toward them, carrying a crowbar.

Suddenly Frances stood over them with something in her hands. For an instant he thought he had been knocked senseless and was losing his mind. She seemed to have a football in her hand—holding it out as though she were getting up a game. Then he heard her screaming to him to run. Did she think he'd leave her and the dog? He looked again. She had raised the gray football up into the air, ready to throw it. Wilson sprang up and ran for the cabin. In a second Frances was behind him, pushing him through the door. A few feet away thousands of wasps were shooting out of their papery nest which now lay in fragments on the driveway. The maddened yellow jackets were charging the two cyclists, savaging them with stings. They dashed for their bikes, screaming and waving their arms around their heads, further infuriating the wasps. In seconds the bikes were racing out of the driveway, the hornets in two tornados behind them.

The minute they were gone, Wilson and Frances ran outside for the dog. He was sitting up, regarding them with a disgusted look on his face. When they called him, the dog walked leisurely toward them, limping slightly. On his way into the cabin he paused to inspect the broken pieces of the hornet's nest. One remaining wasp shot out at him. He snapped it up and swallowed it.

Wilson and Frances sat in front of the fire, the dog next to them, snoring softly, his feet straight up in the air like an upended beetle. Wilson held an old towel packed with ice to the side of his face. The bleeding had stopped, but his eye was swelling shut. Frances sat daubing her hand with ammonia where several wasps had stung her. There was an unspoken agreement between them to dismiss whatever danger they had escaped. Instead, they joked about the panicked flight of the two cyclists. "Can a hornet go faster than a motorcycle?" Wilson asked.

"Oh, I think so, Wilson, when they're very cross. Isn't it a shame Lyle left in such a hurry he didn't have time to put on his helmet. Come to think of it, I might pot up my asparagus fern in it. It would make a nice memento." Her face became serious. "I'm glad you were around tonight."

"It was because of me they came here in the first place. Lyle was mad at something that happened on the rig last night." Then Wilson remembered why he had come to see her. So much had hapepned since the night before that he had nearly forgotten. He decided this was no time to tell her about the well, but she was too quick for him. "I thought you usually went into town on your night off, Wilson?" She waited, eyes narrowed.

Wilson decided he had better tell her. Supposing there was something she could do to stop them from drilling. "Well, I heard the tool pusher talking last night. We're nearly finished drilling on the Janston site and they're planning to come here next."

"Here?"

"They said that their best chance would be up on the bank about a hundred yards from the river. The bottom hole will be under the river, but they'll slant drill."

"That's nonsense, Wilson, they couldn't drill that close to the river. There must be rules about that." She glanced in the direction of the river for collaboration.

He looked embarrassed. "Well, what they said was that because it was *your* property they had checked out all the regulations. If it's state land, you have to keep a quarter mile from water. But if it's private land like yours, there isn't any regulation. They've had the state conservation men out there walking around and checking it out."

For the first time Frances began to take Wilson seriously. She had seen the men from the conservation department on her property last week, but she had thought they were checking the condition of the stream, as they often did. It hadn't occurred to her that they were tramping over her property to see where a well would go, without saying one word to her about it.

Wilson was busy folding and unfolding the dog's ears. He

had not mentioned that Pete said they expected some trouble from the 'old lady who owned the land' but that they could handle her—without mineral rights she didn't have a leg to stand on. "If they do drill here"—Wilson tried to make his voice sound as though it were only a remote possibility, although he knew otherwise—"I wouldn't feel right working on the rig."

"Why not, Wilson?"

"Well, I know how you feel about a well on your land. I don't think I want any part of it."

"On the contrary, Wilson. I can't believe they would ever do it, but if they did, I'd want you there. Maybe you could put some sort of curse on the rig, Wilson, make the drill miss its target." She attempted a smile, but Wilson thought she looked funny, as if she were getting smaller right before his eyes. He was sorry now that he had told her.

After Wilson left, Frances sat by the fire absentmindedly eating the blackberries she had scraped up from the driveway. She enjoyed the contrast of the soft fruity flesh and the little hard seeds, an underrated fruit, she thought, probably because it was so plentiful.

Perhaps the easiest thing to do would be to let them go ahead and drill. Recently she had read that the continents were still slipping and sliding over the earth's surface. If you reckoned time in eons, things got put into their proper perspective. Whatever happened, the land would persevere.

She held up a blackberry she had been about to pop into her mouth and watched a small green worm sway back and forth from its perch on the berry. She opened a window and threw the worm outside. A full moon the color and size of a pumpkin was refracted by the river into glittering orange stripes. She could hear the water as it cascaded over a snagged log.

Taking the flashlight and some newspapers, she went out to cover the tomatoes in case there was a frost. The dog trotted behind her; his limp had disappeared. In the cold air the dog's breath emerged in white puffs. He looked comical, like a trick dog someone had trained to smoke. By the time she finished with the tomatoes, she had mapped her campaign against the oil company. She had had a taste of blood tonight and, with winter coming on, a fight had the smell of life.

14

Mr. Saforth N. Drinnen, President
Ffossco Corporation
Nhelville, Texas

DEAR MR. DRINNEN:

I like to see the people to whom I talk, but since Texas is some distance from here, I must resort to letter writing. However, a letter has the advantage of allowing one to form one's thoughts. I believe much was lost when we put down the pen and took up the telephone.

I cannot in all fairness blame Ffossco for wishing to put an oil well in a promising area. After all, I must be perfectly honest, I drive a truck myself (although not as often as I used to). Also, my home is heated with oil, though I use as little as possible, not, I'm ashamed to say, out of principle but from economy, which sadly, of the two, is often the more convincing taskmaster.

My complaint is that you wish to drill an oil well one hundred yards from one of the loveliest stretches of river in our state. Or anywhere. Appended to my letter you will find a number of photographs which I have taken of the stream over the years. Of course I am an amateur, as you will see at once, but the pictures will show something of what I wish to convey of the river's beauty. (I would appreciate your returning them, as they have been removed from a personal photograph album, hence the torn corners.)

Appended you will find a list of animal and bird inhabitants which I have personally observed in the area where you are proposing to drill. There is also a list of one hundred and sixty-three species of plant life. I must be perfectly honest and admit I have included *Equisetum boreale,* which some consider identical to *Equisetum arvense.* Therefore one could raise a question as to whether it ought to be noted separately.

Finally, our area is full of sinkholes. Your geologists will tell you (perhaps you are one yourself?) that in areas where there are large deposits of limestone bedrock near the surface, rainwater sinking underground slowly dissolves the limestone to form subterranean caverns. Unless the greatest care is taken, natural gas can escape from a well and bubble up through the sinkholes and possibly into the river itself. Surely you will want to reconsider your decision?

Sincerely yours,
Frances Crawford
(Mrs. Thomas C.)

Ffossco Corporation
September 1

Mrs. Thomas C. Crawford
Oclair

Dear Mrs. Crawford:

I am in receipt of your letter of August 30th. Like you, Ffossco is deeply concerned about ecology. Only last month our company gave a substantial grant to a well-known environmental association.

However, our field geologists in your area have assured me

that they are quite certain that the drilling of a well will present no problems.

I am sure that, as a patriotic American, you wish the United States to become as independent as possible from the pressures of foreign governments. America can accomplish this only by a substantial increase in her oil production.

If you have any further questions, our attorney is Archer Preyman, Jr., who has been fully informed of the facts in this case.

Thank you for the very nice photographs, which I am returning.

CORDIALLY,
Sanforth N. Drinnen, President

September 10

Mr. Roger Seaworth, Director
Department of Conservation
8324 Governor Avenue

DEAR MR. SEAWORTH:

I am writing pursuant to my phone call to your department ten days ago, requesting your intervention in the matter of Ffossco Corporation drilling an oil well a hundred yards from the north branch of the Oclair River. Surely your department will not stand by and see the river threatened by possible seepage or spillage. Please let me hear from you at once.

SINCERELY YOURS,
Frances Crawford
(Mrs. Thomas C.)

Mrs. Thomas D. Rawforth
Oclair

DEAR MRS. RAWFORTH:

Rule 321 of the General Rules Governing Oil and Gas Operations sets no limits as to how close a well may be placed in relation to a body of water, unless the land involved is owned by the state, in which case it is unlawful to drill closer than a quarter of a mile to a body of water. Permits to drill are issued by the Geological Survey Department. I would suggest you contact them regarding your other questions.

YOURS TRULY,
Roger Seaworth, Director

September 30

Mrs. Thomas C. Crawford
Oclair

DEAR MRS. CRAWFORD:

A painstaking survey of the geological conditions existing in the prospective drilling area has been completed. I have before me a report from our field geologist. We can say with reasonable certainty that drilling presents little danger to the environment. We see no reason to withdraw the permit we issued to Ffossco. As you know, we have already recommended the drilling site be moved from 100 yards to 300 yards from the river.

The unfortunate incident you mention happened a year ago, and since that time we are enforcing more rigorous standards.

VERY TRULY YOURS,
Lytel Morthman, Director
Geological Survey Department

Governor John Liptonton
992 Executive Office Building
October 12

Mrs. Thomas C. Crawford
Oclair

DEAR MRS. CRAWFORD:

Thank you for the copies of letters which you have exchanged with Ffossco Corporation, the Department of Conservation, and the Office of Geological Surveys.

First let me say I am a great believer in preserving the natural beauty of our great State and I share your concern for the effect of drilling on the ecology. To this end, I have advised all state agencies to exercise the greatest diligence in overseeing the effects of oil production.

I have checked with the appropriate departments regarding the matter on which you express concern, and they have convinced me that all necessary precautions have been taken. I have explained this to State Representative Milton Rudder, who has written me in your behalf.

Your spirited accusation that the state is sympathetic to the oil companies because of the "millions of dollars in oil royalties you have raked in from wells on state land" is unfair. The interests of the State are at all times the same as the interests of its citizens. All royalties are placed directly in the general fund of the State Treasury, where they are appropriately disbursed. Only a small percentage goes for what you choose to call "the inflated salaries of incompetent bureaucrats."

I welcome your concern and appreciate your bringing this matter to my attention, and I look forward to visiting your lovely section of the State in the near future.

WITH EVERY GOOD WISH I AM,
John Liptonton, Governor

Department of Conservation
Department of Geological Survey
Representative Milton Rudder

October 12

Mrs. Thomas Crawford
Oclair

DEAR MRS. CRAWFORD:

As sympathetic as we are to your plight, we unfortunately do not have the manpower to give our attention to individual cases. It may be of some comfort to you to know that TREE itself has allowed drilling in its bird sanctuary, which is located only a few miles from you. The funds accruing from these wells have been of inestimable help in carrying out our crusade for good conservation practices.

A membership blank is enclosed.

SINCERELY YOURS,
Ward Simon Smithe,
Executive Secretary

Ralston Clifter
Counselor at Law
761 Oak Street
Oclair
October 21

Mrs. Thomas C. Crawford
Oclair

DEAR FRANCES,

I am having my secretary, Betty Jean, return the file of letters you dropped off at the office the other day while I was at Rotary. I was sorry to have missed you. I'm afraid since Tom went, Elsie and I haven't seen as much of you as we would like. Elsie is going to give you a ring real soon.

As you know, I have always been glad to handle any legal work for you and Tom (after all, I figure I owe my life to Tom), however, in this case I'm afraid I cannot help you, as I am on a retainer to Ffossco Corporation and serve as their attorney in this area.

Frankly, as an old friend of the family, my advice would be to trust Ffossco in this matter. I am sure you will find them more than decent once they know you wish to cooperate with them.

WITH BEST REGARDS,
Ral

c.c. Ffossco Corporation
Nehlville, Texas

Kevin Loft, Attorney
North Branch Plaza
Oclair
October 29

Ms. Thomas C. Crawford
Oclair

DEAR MS. CRAWFORD:

I was pleased to receive your letter. I share your concern for the environment, and your case is just the kind I have been looking for since moving here two months ago. Nothing is closer to my heart than the welfare of our beautiful woods and waters.

Although I am just starting out, I know that it is important for attorney and client to understand exactly what is involved in "going to law." Ffossco has the services of a full-time legal staff available to them, as well as their own geological experts. We, of course, would have to hire such experts. Furthermore precedent has favored the rights of owners of mineral rights over owners of surface rights. I am perfectly willing to help you, but win or loose, it is only fair that you understand that the cost to you may be considerable.

I am looking forward to hearing from you on this matter in the near future.

SINCERELY YOURS,
Kevin North

Pine County State Bank
45 Maine Street
Oclair
November 2

Dear Frances,

I am sorry to tell you it will not be possible for the bank to increase your mortgage. I've known you a long enough time to come right out and say that you have had difficulty in meeting your present payments. In addition, property values where owners do not have mineral rights have declined due to the proliferation of wells, so that our evaluation of your property at this time would be downward.

If the decision were mine alone, you know I would be glad to oblige, but I am accountable to the bank's investors.

Hoping to be of service in the future,
Ralph

Ralston Clifter
Counselor at Law
761 Oak Street
Oclair
November 12

Mrs. Thomas C. Crawford
Oclair

Dear Mrs. Crawford:

The Ffossco Corporation has asked me as their legal representative in this area to write to you regarding several questionable incidents occurring during the past weeks. On November 4th the company crew found a tree had been cut down in such a manner as to block a road they have constructed to a well site on your property. This was repeated on two further occasions. Holes have been dug in the road and nails and other sharp devices have been scattered about in the path of trucks. Valuable construction material was discovered in the river. This has resulted in considerable delay and expense to my client.

Furthermore, signs posted on your property such as "KEEP OFF," "SET GUNS," and "WATCH OUT FOR LAND MINES" are considered to be undue harassment. If you do not cease and desist, legal action will be taken forthwith.

Frances, for God's sake, this is no laughing matter. The company has gone through due process and is within its legal rights in drilling on your property. As you well know. They are losing patience and a lot of money by the delay and think you are some kind of looney. The next step is unquestionably a warrant for your arrest.

SINCERELY,
Ralston

Frances put the letter down. Jail. Who would feed the dog?

15

When Wilson's alarm rang at five in the morning, its obstreperous jangling drove him under the covers. For several minutes nothing in the world seemed more important than the warmth of his bed. It was a snug boat pitching on the uncertain sea of a new day and he clung to it.

Gradually he let himself become interested in why he was getting up so early. It was the first day of the hunting season. The November sky was black. Although the temperature must have fallen down into the twenties, there was no snow on the ground. Hunters would be tracking their deer over brittle leaves and dried bracken, and the deer would hear them come. He had another plan.

Encouraged by the smell of coffee and bacon ascending the stairway, he began to pull on his clothes. If the house were burning, his mother would make them all eat a big breakfast before she let them escape to safety.

His dad, hunched over a bowl of oatmeal, asked where he was hunting.

Wilson hesitated over his father's question, busying himself with the plate of buckwheat cakes gilded with butter and syrup that his mother placed in front of him. Everything felt so good this morning, the warmth and light of the kitchen, the food, the excitement of a day's hunting ahead of him. He didn't want to spoil it by telling them he was going to hunt on Frances Crawford's property. But if he didn't, his dad might notice where Wilson parked the truck or one of his dad's friends might run into him.

A week ago there had been a big fight. Because his parents were so opposed to his going to college, he had given Frances's address instead of his own when he sent out his applications. When he had received an acceptance from Northern, where there was one of the best geological departments anywhere, he had brought his acceptance home so he could take it out and look at it whenever he wanted to. His mom had come across it cleaning his rooms and had showed it to his dad.

They had been furious. "That's a sneaky thing to do, Wilson," his dad had said, "and there isn't going to be any more of it. What does that old lady think she's up to?"

His mother had even blamed Frances for his working on the rig. "I remember how she came by that day you went to Oclair to apply for the job and picked you up in her truck right in front of our house, bold as brass."

"She's been nothing but trouble for you, Wilson," his dad had said, "Don't tell me you wouldn't have gotten all beat up by those motorcyclists if you hadn't been over there. As long as you're living in this house, I don't want to hear of you going to her place again."

And for the last few days Wilson had stayed away from Frances's. Should his parents kick him out, he would have to use his money for board and room and he'd never be able to save enough for school. If he could just hold on until next fall he'd be all right. But he had no intention of not seeing Frances, though he supposed he'd have to find a way of doing it without letting his folks know. But today was another matter.

"Well, Mrs. Crawford said I could hunt on her property."

His father put down his coffee cup and his mother gave the potatoes a violent stir. He hurried on, "I know what you're thinking, but just this once. It's the best place in the county to hunt. She's never let anyone hunt there before. I wouldn't have to talk to her or anything."

He could see his dad struggle between meat on the table and his feelings about Frances. The meat won.

Wilson moved quietly along the trail that led into the Crawford property, hoping he wouldn't spook the buck before daybreak, when the hunting season officially opened. About twenty feet into the woods from the trail, he had built a blind of pine branches. He squeezed himself into the opening and settled down on the frozen ground, enjoying the rich scent of the pine and feeling snug in the seclusion of the blind. Before choosing the site, he had spent days tracking the big buck. A short distance from the site he had found a "scrape," a shallow circular depression in the ground made by the buck pawing at the earth and urinating to mark it as his territory. It was a warning to other bucks to stay away. November was the mating season and the buck didn't want any interference with his does.

Wilson had felt a little guilty about going after the big buck. Not that he took Frances's warning seriously, but because he thought she half believed it. He was not sure why she had allowed him to hunt on her property. Of course he had promised her meat, but he felt the real reason was that she had seen how he had grown to accept much of what she believed about the land—and this was his reward.

It was a fair contest, Wilson told himself. The buck knew all the paths. His smell and hearing and eyesight were superior to Wilson's. The buck could run thirty miles an hour and his color was a perfect camouflage. Often the only glimpse you had of him against the brown foliage was the inside of a leg or the flick of his white tail.

Wilson settled down into the blind, feeling well provisioned. His down jacket, the same one he used on the rig, was warm and light. His boots and gloves had foam insulation. Hooked onto his belt was a sheath knife that had once belonged to Dr.

Crawford; it had a rosewood handle with brass rivets and a sharp stainless steel blade. In a pocket were sandwiches. Next to him was the gun that had killed the fawn. He felt that if he could kill the buck in a fair contest, it would erase his unhappy associations with the gun.

Gray light began to separate earth from sky. Maneuvering slowly, Wilson picked up the rifle and swung it from side to side to be sure it cleared the branches of the blind. Then he settled down to wait. In the distance he heard other hunters rushing loudly through the woods, trying to scare the deer and get them running toward their buddies who were waiting to get a shot.

As the morning dragged on, he heard rifle fire two or three times. He became impatient. The cold dampness of the ground began to leech through his clothes. His arms and legs were cramped from the long hours of sitting. By noon the woods were perfectly still and Wilson knew most of the hunters would have returned to their camps, some with their bucks, but most with stories of the big one that got away.

Wilson was ready to leave, for you seldom saw deer this time of day. Deer browse for their feed in early morning, swallowing ten to fifteen pounds of twigs and leaves; their work done for the day, they find a sunny, well-protected spot and for the next several hours lay quietly chewing their cuds.

As Wilson prepared to leave, there was movement on the trail. He froze. Two does stepped along. Ten yards behind them came the buck, his magnificent rack of antlers silhouetted against the sky. Wilson sighted a spot just in back of the buck's shoulder, hesitated for a second, then pressed the trigger. After his rifle went off he heard a dull thunking sound that told him the bullet had hit home. The buck swung his head in Wilson's direction, then turned into the woods.

Wilson raced after him. He remembered the legend of the Indian hunters. But the buck did not lead him deep into the woods. A hundred yards or so from the trail, Wilson found him, legs crumbled under his body. He was dead.

Wilson stood over him. There were pink splotches of blood

on his chest; probably he had died from a lung shot. The antlers had ten points. Though Wilson had run only a short distance, he was breathing hard and his hands were trembling. Taking out his knife, he began to gut the buck. It was a job he hated and got through only because there was a certain satisfaction in doing it correctly. Once the buck was eviscerated, heart, lungs and stomach all removed, it seemed to Wilson the buck's spirit had passed away and no longer could run off into the woods and life.

16

Frances heard the first shot only minutes after sunrise. On chilly mornings like this she woke to find her hands drawn into rigid claws; each finger had to be painfully stretched out and wiggled into usefulness. The room was cold, and getting out of bed required cajolery and petty bribes—promises to herself of second cups of coffee and the further postponement of any housecleaning. She pulled on warm wool slacks and an old sweater. Because Wilson had said that if he got his deer he would stop by, she tied on a bright parsley-green scarf.

The dog, in a fit of excessive morning enthusiasm, rushed to the door ahead of Frances, nearly knocking her over. While she searched through the closet for his red coat, put away at the end of last year's hunting season, he whined impatiently to be let out. He was just the size and color of a small deer and she didn't take chances. Each year dogs, cows and people were mistaken for deer and shot. In the afternoon she would walk down to the mailbox, wearing a red cap and ringing a cowbell, enjoying the expression on the faces of any hunters she met.

Settled in front of the kitchen window with a large mug of coffee, she stared gloomily out at the colorless river merging with the colorless sky; even the feathers of the few goldfinches that came to the feeder had molted from bright yellow to an olive drab. The winter hunger for color was upon her.

It was not only the drab winter landscape that distressed her. Upstream from the cabin, the oak, jackpine and birch had been cut down. In their place a derrick of red steel, with supports like giant cross stitches, rose into the air. Beside the derrick the one remaining tree, a pine that once had seemed a giant, now appeared insignificant.

A week ago she had walked over to talk to the men who were beginning to clear the site for the oil rig. She had been furious with them for being on her land, doubly furious because she didn't have the right to throw them off. But she wanted something, and to get it she knew she would have to control her anger.

As soon as they saw her, bulldozer, chain saws, trucks, everything, had come to a halt. Just like the mural on the post office wall, she had thought, with its frieze of muscular lumbermen interrupted in the middle of cutting down a painted forest. Why were the men staring at her? Did they expect her to twine herself fanatically about a tree trunk and dare them to cut it down. She had called out, "Which one of you is the boss?"

No one had moved. Fright or egalitarianism?

"Somebody is surely in charge here."

One of the men had stepped forward. He wore wire-rimmed glasses and had the slightly near-sighted look of someone who checked blueprints or corrected papers. Except for the fact that he was splotched from head to foot with mud, he could have been a draftsman or an English teacher. "What can we do for you, Ma'am?"

"I want to know exactly which trees of mine you plan to cut down."

"We're only going to clear a space big enough for the rig, about three acres, couple thousand trees or so. All the poplars, most of the jackpine, those oak trees over there, and the big

Norway. Oh, and the birch." He looked at the other men for support, but they were looking at her.

No one reached the age of eighty without plenty of experience in the art of relinquishment, but the Norway rose into the air like the spar of a windjammer. In the evening its dense shape was weightier than the darkness. She shoved a book under the man's nose. "This is a history of Pine County. I hope you recognize the pine tree in the photograph on the cover. You start to fool around with that tree and I'll get the County Board of Supervisors up here." The pine on the cover was one that grew three miles away, but the man wouldn't know that.

He studied the picture. "Well . . ." Turning to the operator of the bulldozer, he asked, "What about if we leave that corner there where the pine is and they can squeeze the tanks over in this direction?"

The operator shrugged.

The man turned back to her. "But the other trees got to go. We're already keeping the space more tight than we should. It's for your own protection, ma'am. If a fire gets going, you dont' want any trees close by."

She remembered the red glow in the sky last spring and nodded.

Then the frieze of men came to life. Bulldozers rumbled back and forth for three days, shouldering down the trees; only the largest were accorded the dignity of being individually felled. They were cut down on the second day. She had sat in the cabin listening to the whine of the chain saws. By five o'clock she could see a pile of logs heaped up high as a house, all cut into two-foot lengths. A half hour later when she looked again, they were gone.

She was out of the house and into her pickup. It took her nearly ten minutes to catch up with the big truck, but once she saw it, she gained on it steadily. It was big and cumbersome and the heavy load of logs slowed it down. Steal her trees, would they! She passed it on the crest of a hill, edging an oncoming car and its terrified driver off onto the shoulder. Once in front of the truck, she screeched to a halt, blocking its path.

She jumped out and stamped over to the two men in the cab, who looked down at her and listened to what she had to say with stupified expressions. For many years they had worked with tough men, doing rough work. They had struggled with frozen equipment in below zero weather and once they had spent the better part of a day pulling a capsized trailer out of a mud bank in the rain, but even in their extremity they had not had recourse to so rich a vocabulary. The summary of Frances's various suggestions and remarks was that they should turn their truck around forthwith and deliver the logs to her cabin door.

When they arrived, they found her plans for them included stacking the wood. Otherwise, she told them, the sheriff would be called in. ("My good friend, the sheriff" was how she had put it.) There were eight cords of wood, and they finished stacking it by moonlight. When they were through, she gave them each a glass of cider and told them they had done a nice job.

After that, the crew was never out of her sight. Each morning she measured the distance to the river with a ball of string to be sure they had not edged closer.

In the daytime, when the bulldozing crew was there in front of her and she could confront the enemy, it was tolerable; in the evening, when they were gone and she stood looking across the three acres that had once been forest and were now nothing more than a flat stretch of naked sand, she was desolate and could think of nothing to say to the river.

Then the derrick took over the empty space. For days trucks rolled in and out, dragging long trailers loaded with lengths of steel. What had once been a footpath through the woods became a roadway thirty feet wide. An enormous ditch stood ready to hold the brine and drilling compound. Another ditch was excavated for innumerable black plastic bags of cans and paper that seemed to accumulate endlessly. At one end of the clearing two house trailers had been set up.

The dog was delighted with all the activity. Each morning he was anxious to be out on his rounds of the location and had long since made friends with the drillers. He begged scraps shamelessly from their lunch each noon, and in the evening when Wilson arrived for the night shift, he bounded over to greet him.

Finally, two days ago, at four in the morning, the engines had been switched on and the drilling began. Sometimes the sound of the engines was like a surf rolling in; at other times there was an urgent bleating noise, accompanied by black puffs of smoke. More irritating than the noise was the suspense. If they found oil, the site would be enlarged and a moonscape of holding tanks, pumps and heaters would go up. Day and night, machinery would run and oil tankers would lumber in and out.

Because he knew how anxious Frances was, Wilson had managed to be assigned to the rig so that he could report to her. He did it with a high sense of drama, calling in from obscure phone booths and lowering his voice as though someone might be following him. The men who worked on the rig weren't supposed to give out any information which might alert other oil companies with property nearby. He had told her that if his calls were discovered, he could lose his job. What he hadn't told her was that much of his secrecy was to keep his parents from knowing that he was still in touch with her.

Early in the afternoon Frances heard a truck pull into her road. Since the dog wasn't barking, she guessed it was Wilson. He climbed out of the front seat, grinning. From the doorway she watched him heave the carcass of a deer out of the back of the pickup.

She saw from the size of its antlers that it was the old buck. She told herself there was no point in mourning his passing. The herd was large this year. They were predicting a bad winter with the kind of snow that immobilized deer. Certainly a shot was better than slow starvation. She consoled herself with Wilson's triumphant look and the thought of how good a haunch of venison would taste. But with the buck dead, she wondered who would help her watch over the land.

17

When she looked out of the window and saw the snow whipping into migrating drifts, Wilson's mother begged him to stay home. "Call them and tell them you're not feeling well," she said.

But Wilson could imagine what T. K.'s response would be to that. "First little bit of weather we get and the boy cops out," he'd say. "When you goin' to hire on some real men, Pete?" If the weather was bad tonight, it would be a lot worse before the winter was over. Once they started drilling a well, they didn't stop until they finished. The rig cost thousands of dollars a day; to let it stand idle would have been wasteful. It ran twenty-four hours a day, twelve months a year.

When Wilson reached the site, the earlier shift was leaving. "Don't envy you," one of the men called out to him. "That pipe's colder than a well-digger's bottom." Wilson's heart sank when he saw they hadn't finished sending the pipe down and his shift would have to complete the job, struggling with the cold metal in the snow and high winds.

Pete sent Wilson up to the platform. "You can start off up there," he told him. "If it gets too bad, holler, and I'll send Barch up to trade off with you."

Wilson fastened on his safety line and slowly made his way up the snow-covered scaffolding. Climbing the open ladder was bad, but riding the block up was worse. You stood there suspended from the giant steel weight, moving unprotected through the air.

He eased himself onto the platform's slippery metal slats. The wind and snow slashed at his face. Snow accumulated in heavy flakes on his eyelashes, making it difficult to see, and fell on his nose and mouth. He ran his tongue around his lips and tasted the snow. In other years the first big snowfall had been reason for celebration; in this work it was nothing but a nuisance.

A hundred feet below, Lyle, manipulating the drawworks, had sent the block shooting up through the derrick's open center, and Wilson reached out to attach the first piece of pipe. The block was barely within reach. Wilson had to stretch dangerously close to the edge of the platform. Since he had been chased off of Mrs. Crawford's property, Lyle had done everything he could to make Wilson's work as difficult and dangerous as possible. Wilson thought Lyle suspected him of telling Pete and T. K. about the hornet's nest. He hadn't. Even when Lyle had turned up at work covered with red welts, Wilson had said nothing. Maybe that was what had really angered Lyle: Wilson's silence. It gave him a kind of power over Lyle.

Wilson shook the snow from the top of the pipe and made the connection. In weather like this everything took twice as long. They wouldn't be breaking any records tonight. Wilson's first half hour on the platform seemed like a week. He thought of calling down and exchanging jobs, but he didn't want to give Lyle the satisfaction of seeing him give up.

From his perch on the platform, the river below him was little more than a black ribbon winding between the white, snow-covered banks. He thought of how different it had looked a few months ago and remembered a day in August when he had fished one of the small feeder streams. To take his mind off of the wind and snow, he tried to summon back the summer afternoon.

The wet sand along the low edges of the bank had been covered with a filigree of woodcock tracks and tunneled with muskrat holes. There were spikes of scarlet cardinal flower and the grass-of-Parnassus was just starting to bloom. Where the land had been burned off, silt had washed into the stream and the water all but disappeared. He had to wade through swales of tall sedges, soft mud sucking at his feet.

Water striders swam upstream in little jerks, stopped, and were carried downstream again, each time gaining half again as much distance as they had lost. Their shadows moved with them like black flowers, each one with a large center and four smaller surrounding petals.

It was nearly impossible to cast without snagging his line in the tag alder and willow branches that stretched like a green canopy over his head. The trout here were small and wary, skittering off at the least movement.

Behind him he saw how the path he had made through the tall marsh grass allowed the current to flow more quickly. In the small feeder streams, unlike the river, where a hundred men coming and going would make little difference, one person passing through the tiny creek could cause an irreversible change. For this reason the small stream seemed more human than the river, more vulnerable.

About twenty feet upstream a cloud-shaped mass moved over the water. It was nearly ten feet across, much larger than a swarm of bees. It dipped over the stream, rose, and dipped again. He hurried to investigate. As he got closer, he could see the cloud was made up of shiny green fragments, thousands of migrating dragonflies—green darners. They were driven by an instinct that made no sense. He knew dragonflies rarely migrated. They would die before the season was over, so why did they bother to leave their breeding ground? The shimmering green cloud bannered out and disappeared, leaving him with the loneliness of one who had seen a vision—something that no one could ever share with him.

A cold gust of wind scattered the images of the summer's day and Wilson, feeling the sharp chill of the steel through his gloves, swung out the last length of pipe. He started down the ladder, only to find it was nearly impossible for him to keep his balance on the snow-packed rungs. He would never be able to make his way down. Below him through the white streaks of snow, he saw Pete wave his arms and motion toward the block. Wilson guessed he was telling him not to try decending the ladder but to ride the block down.

When it reached the platform, Wilson forced himself into the open elevator that dangled from the block. It was like standing up in a swing one hundred feet in the air. The snow and wind came at him from all sides, each flake highlighted in the glare of the floodlights. Below him he could make out T. K.'s red parka and Lyle at the drawworks controlling his descent. From this height they looked like midgets.

It seemed to him that Lyle was bringing him down too fast. He felt himself dropping toward earth as though someone had pushed him out of a window or the door of an airplane. He was nearly even with the roof of the doghouse and he waited for Lyle to slow the block down, but the ground rushed toward him. Then it slammed against his body.

18

In the early hours of that November morning Frances dreamed she was walking in the deep forest where the thick trees screened out the sun. Enormous white triangular forms sprang up in front of her. They were the skeletons of icebergs, their bones ice-encrusted steel. A wintery gale pushed and tugged at the huge shapes until they began to sway and groan. Animals raced past her to escape the teetering giants. As the winds howled, the skeletons crashed to the ground, one by one, crushing the fleeing animals beneath them. It was their frightened screams that awakened her. Then the animals shrieks became a siren—something real.

Frances extricated herself from the tangle of sheets and blankets she had woven with her tossing and turning. The siren was coming from the well site. The lights of the rig were visible through the white snow that sliced the black sky. Her first thought was that the well had caught fire. She looked for flames rising in the darkness, but there was only the usual cold white glare of the fluorescent lights that made the site look like an operating room. The sirens faded. Since Wilson was working on the night shift, he'd be able to tell her what had happened.

Although it was only six o'clock, she dressed hurriedly, anxious to get out of the room where she felt that pieces of her nightmare were still bumping about in the darkness. There was a lovely early-morning farm program from the state college on television. The people appearing on the program were exactly like the people she used to know fifty years ago. Only their clothing had changed.

Frances turned on the porch light before letting the dog out and saw a huge gray shape leave the ground, circle the cabin, and fly away. A small mangled animal lay a few feet from the door; beneath it the snow was red. An owl had been tearing at something. For the last week the tracks of a snowshoe hare had cut through the yard. Last night she had thrown out some old apples and greens for the hare. Instead of it having been a kindness, she had made the hare move into the dangerous open space where an owl had been watching.

Stupid and thoughtless she had been. The trouble was that in winter she felt deserted when raccoons and porcupines curled up in trees and snakes and worms twined together underground. There was nothing for company but birds.

She scolded herself for sounding like a petulant old lady. She had her books, and Wilson managed to stop by each week. Together they were charting the drill's progress as it passed through shale, where cold water was trapped in pools, down into rock that had once been covered by inland seas, and into the salt beds. Wilson had brought some of the salt for her. It had given her a strange feeling to taste salt from her own land and know that it was millions of years old. "Don't worry," Wilson kept assuring her, "they aren't going to find any oil. I won't let them."

She settled down in front of the television set with a cup of coffee. The dog lay beside her, gnawing idly on the leg of the chair. The farm program today was on beekeeping. Unsettling closeups of the insects turned them into huge furry animals.

She refilled her coffee cup and listened to the morning news, read by newscasters natty in red blazers with the station's crest in gold on their pockets. Plans were announced for a cross-country ski-athon later in the winter. The first snow-storm of the season had resulted in a delay of several school buses. The announcer shuffled his papers. "An accident occurred early this morning at a Ffossco well site, located in Pine County. A young man working at the site was seriously hurt in a fall. It is not known at this time what caused the accident. The name of the injured man is Wilson Catchner, believed to be a resident of Pine County."

Frances threw on her coat. Her boots were buried some-where in the pile of winter clothing on the floor of the closet. She left without them, and as she hurried to the truck, the wet snow crept into her shoes and chilled her feet. The accident was her fault! She remembered how Wilson had wanted to quit and she had encouraged him to stay. She prayed that he would be all right, falling back for some reason on a childhood prayer that she hadn't thought of for seventy years.

The truck moved hesitantly through the drifts, resisting her efforts to gun it over the slippery rises. The wiper didn't seem to be working; in order to see the road, she had to stop every few minutes to clear off the windshield.

At seven-thirty the sky was still dark, the shapes of the snow-covered houses along the road a ghostly white. A snow-plow loomed up in front of her. It was impossible to see beyond it in order to pass. The snow from its blade was thrown against the truck, encrusting the windshield with snow. The ride seemed endless. Nearly an hour later when she reached the hospital, its rows of lighted rooms in the darkened city suggested a terrible urgency. The parking lot was familiar. In the last years of Tom's illness she had often driven him there so that he could see his patients.

She hurried inside. A nurse was walking in and out of the patients' rooms, dispensing medication from tiny paper cups arranged neatly on a metal tray. An aide rattled a cart of breakfast trays past her. Frances looked for a familiar face, but everyone was a stranger.

When she reached the large swinging door that led into the

emergency room, she stopped, afraid to go farther. Only her need to see Wilson finally gave her the courage to push open the door.

Mr. and Mrs. Catchner were standing beside the nurse's desk. They looked defenseless and out of place, like civilians caught by an invading army. She started toward them, relieved to see that the nurse at the desk was Lou Walsh, whom she had known for years. Before she could say a word, the Catchners saw her and moved close to each another, forming a wall between her and Lou's desk.

Mrs. Catchner's voice was sharp: "I don't think you have any business to be here, Mrs. Crawford."

Frances tried to answer, but it was like groping about in a dark bag to try to find the right words. "I just wanted to see Wilson—to find out how he is." Then, acknowledging their prior claim as his parents, she hastily added: "If it's all right with you."

Mr. Catchner's face was red, his voice loud in the hushed hospital room: "Don't you think you've caused enough trouble? If it weren't for you giving Wilson grand ideas about going to college, none of this would have happened!"

Frances was not hurt. Hadn't she had already accused herself of the same thing? The phone on Lou Walsh's desk rang. Then she motioned the Catchners to follow her. She glanced back apologetically at Frances.

Frances watched them disappear. She considered running after them, but knew she would be turned back. She thought of remaining until they returned, but could not bear to face them again. She fled.

All day long she sat in front of the television set, hoping for news of Wilson. One daytime serial followed another. Their artificial tales of woe seemed to Frances a mockery of her anguish. A game show came on. The master of ceremonies was a fatherly man proudly showing off the contestants as if they were his bright children. A young couple stood at the microphone. The woman was jumping up and down, squealing with excitement; her husband continually slapped his forehead. Every few minutes the couple threw themselves into each other's arms with obviously feigned excitement.

Frances got up from her chair and carried her cup of cold coffee into the kitchen. The snowstorm had stopped. It was dark now, but a full moon cast a pale glow on the snow-covered ground. From the window she could make out the carcass of the hare. She thought of the owl returning in the night, circling the cabin, nervous in the bright light of the full moon. It would settle on the hare and try to tear off some meat, but the hare's body would be frozen into a solid lump. The owl would hunch patiently over the hare, waiting for the warmth of its body to thaw the carcass. Then it would begin to rip off pink ribbons of the hare's flesh.

She searched through the cupboard. On a shelf next to a box of old cookie cutters and a bag of dead light bulbs she found some rat poison. She would make slits in the frozen body of the hare and insert the poison. The owl would do no more killing. But before she could carry out her plan, a dark shape appeared against the moon.

It was a great gray owl, rare in that part of the country: *Scoliaptex nebulosa,* the Greek eagle-owl of darkness. The owl was the white-gray color of a winter morning, its breast soft and thick with down. The great gray owl had been sighted flying across Lapland and Russia and Mongolia. It was the largest of the owls. For revenge she had nearly murdered a king. For the first time that day she began to cry.

A pair of headlights appeared on the trail and the owl flew off. It was the Catchners' truck. For a minute Frances expected to see Wilson climb out and make his way up the walk, but it was his father who knocked at her door. She urged him to come into the cabin, but he refused her invitation with a quick shake of his head.

"I guess he's going to make it," was all he said, and then he turned on his heel and headed for the truck. The headlights swung in an arc and disappeared.

Frances went out into the yard, forgetting to put on a coat. She hacked at the frozen earth with a shovel until she had a hole large enough to bury the hare. She laid it gently into the ground and covered it over. As she finished, a shadow winged silently across the snow. The great gray owl circled the yard, once, twice, and flew off carrying its shadow with it.

19

In the third week of December an unseasonable rain fell. Drops of water clung to the bottoms of the tree branches. By early afternoon the temperature suddenly fell, and the drops stretched into icicles. The trunks of the trees were glazed, their ice-encrusted branches bent nearly to the ground. Frances shouted to the wet birds gathered on the feeder to go home, but some primal knowledge of how hard it would be to find food with all the vegetation iced over kept them there eating compusively, stopping only long enough to fluff up bedraggled feathers.

At five minutes past five, the electric clock stopped. The furnace died, and the lights went off. She wondered if a tree limb, heavy with ice, had fallen on the power line. She could still hear the whining roar of the oil drill. Nothing seemed to stop the drilling. She looked through windows glazed with ice. The lights on the rig were on. They must have their own generator, she decided.

When she opened the door to go out for firewood, she heard a sharp crack as the ice sealing the door split. One look at the slick sidewalk made her think better of going outside. What if she fell and broke a leg? Who would find her? The dog ran past her, spreading his paws to give him more traction on the ice, but when all four legs slid out from under him, he turned around and came back in, avoiding her gaze.

She closed off the rest of the house, drained the pipes in the bathroom and kitchen so they wouldn't freeze when the cold began to fill the house, and started a small fire in the fireplace. Sometimes the power stayed out for a couple of days. In a way it was pleasant, this containment within a small center of warmth by the fireplace, with nothing to do. These last weeks since Wilson's accident, the simplest thing had been an effort.

After the confrontation with his parents, she had been afraid to return to the hospital. Instead, she had gone into town nearly every day so that she could use the phone to call Lou Walsh and find out how Wilson was. He had been badly shaken up, but mercifully, Lou had told her, no bones had been broken. Their greatest concern had been the possibility of a head injury. There had been headaches and for a few days a memory loss, but gradually these symptoms had cleared up. The day before yesterday Lou had told her that Wilson had been doing so well he had been allowed to go home.

Driving by the Catchners' house on her way home from town, Frances had peered through the lighted windows, hoping against hope for a glimpse of Wilson, but the living room, which faced the road, had been empty. She would probably never see Wilson at her cabin again, but that was a small price to pay for his recovery.

She slept for a while, waking to a cold dark room. The fire was out. She fed a little of the wood that remained into the dwindling blue flames and lighted a kerosene lamp. Her world had shrunk to a circle of pale yellow light. Familiar objects looked strange. She might be in someone else's room. It was the shadows, she decided, the way they concealed certain things that had been visible.

She knew she ought to eat some dinner, but she couldn't bring herself to leave the warmth of the fire for the cold kitchen. She ate less and less these days. As soon as she thought of food, she thought perversely past the point of its edibility, imagining bread green with mold, butter rancid, meats tinged with putrescent green; even a fresh red apple tasted of soft brown spots and wormholes. She blew out the lamp to conserve kerosene, crept deeper into a coat she had put on that had once belonged to Tom and was long enough to reach down to her feet, and fell asleep. She dreamed she was picking berries in the middle of winter, reaching up high into bare black branches for fruit red as blood. As she bent the branches, she could hear the sheath of ice that coated the twigs breaking into shards. The juice from the fruit covered her thick wool gloves and formed a frozen sugary crust along the edges of her pail.

She awakened to a bright sky. At first she thought the lights had gone on, then she realized she had slept through the night and into the morning. Each ice-glazed tree glowed red, blue, and yellow in the sunlight, a feast of primary colors. Light glanced off the crust of ice that covered the snow. The view from the windows was dazzling.

The fire had died during the night and every joint in her chilled body was stiff, the least movement painful. She was weak and lightheaded from not eating and had to hang onto the backs of chairs to get across the room. Years ago in the state mental hospital they had "untidy wards," and she thought how well she would fit into one, with her wispy uncombed hair, twisted stockings and crumbled clothes. She understood the senile old women rocking madly in their chairs and shouting out obscenities. A time came when you were sick and tired of your body's needs—shoveling in food, clipping nails, combing hair. Once you interrupted the routine, it was difficult to think of a reason to resume it.

She settled into an armchair, legs tucked under her, and warmed by the sun she floated in and out of consciousness. The dog had resigned himself to staying inside. She had managed a trip into the kitchen to open a bag of dog kibble for him, but it had slipped out of her hands, spilling over the floor, and she had left it. Whatever happened to her, he would have enough food.

Late in the day the sun disappeared and snow fell in thick silent flakes. Watching it made her dizzy. With the sun's warmth gone from the room, an icy numbness touched her hands and feet. She clenched her teeth to keep them from chattering. Her whole body was shivering uncontrollably. She padded across the chilly floor to the fireplace and reached out shaky hands to pick up a log. Its weight surprised her, tipping her off balance. She fell against a chair, sinking into a darkness beyond the darkness of the room. Once, she awoke to feel an animal warmth against her, a rise and fall of heavy breathing. She tried to remember where she was, but there seemed to be no clues—only darkness. A moment later she drifted off again into the warmth of sleep.

20

Wilson had been home from the hospital for two days when the lawyer arrived. It was Wilson's first day out of bed, and after the confinement of the hospital and his bedroom, just walking through the house to the kitchen was a trip to a new country. His mother had wanted to keep him in bed longer, but by managing the enormous task of eating everything she cooked for him, Wilson had convinced her he was much improved.

T. K. had visited him nearly every day in the hospital, almost unrecognizable in a blue suit, pink shirt, and red tie. Only the old high-heeled, mud-splotched boots were familiar. Once he had come bearing a potted plant, holding it gingerly as if he suspected it might climb out of its pot and do something erratic. On the accompanying card were the signatures of all the men who had worked with Wilson on the rig.

It was T. K. who had told him that Ffossco meant to "do something" for him. Wilson had not understood what that meant, thinking that perhaps they were going to send him a plant, too. T. K. also told him that Lyle Barch had been fired. Someone had seen him heading downstate on his motorcycle, a suitcase strapped to the carrier.

The lawyer was Ralston Clifter, a member of their church. When he arrived at the door, the Catchners thought he was making a churchly visit. But Ralston Clifter carried a briefcase, and by the way he refused a cup of coffee and sat stiffly in his chair, they guessed the visit was official.

"I'm certainly glad to see how well you're looking, Wilson," Clifter said. "That was a most unfortunate accident." He emphasized the word "accident."

"I'm not sure it was an accident," Wilson said.

Clifter, appearing not to hear him, hurried on. "I want you to know Ffossco will take care of your medical expenses. As their legal representative in Oclair, naturally I want to see that the people who live here get every consideration."

Mr. Catchner, who had been looking rather puzzled, now leaned forward like a fisherman who thinks he has snagged an old tin can and, instead, reels in a big fish.

"What I'm proposing—" Clifter carefully removed from his briefcase a sheaf of neatly typed pages arranged into three little bundles, each tucked into a blue folder—"what I'm proposing is that Ffossco take care of all your medical expenses and in addition—" He lingered over the word "addition," as though it were a particularly tasty morsel—"we will give you the sum of five thousand dollars for any, ah, inconvenience the accident might have caused you."

Wilson was elated. Since the accident he had given up the hope of college, knowing his parents wouldn't let him return to the rig. With what he had saved, the five thousand dollars would let him start school.

But his father was scowling. He leaned toward the lawyer. "Inconvenience? Hell, that boy just about had himself killed!"

Clifter concentrated on arranging the little bundles of paper from one neat pile into another. "Well, it's conceivable we might go a *little* higher, though you ought to know expenses for that particular well have been way over the estimate and they just learned today that there was no pay—it's a dry well. They've packed up the rig and pulled out."

"That well may be dry," Wilson's dad said, "but there's plenty of Ffossco wells that aren't."

Wilson stopped listening to the two men. Would Mrs. Crawford know the river was safe? Probably in this ice storm there was no way for her to get over and check the well each day.

They were looking at Wilson now, and Clifter was laying the bundles of paper in front of him and handing him a pen. Wilson looked at his dad, who nodded approval. On each bundle was a place for Wilson's signature. There was also an inked line through the sum of five thousand dollars. Written over it was the sum of ten thousand dollars, and next to the new amount were Clifter's initials, neat as the three bundles.

Wilson's parents stood behind him while he carefully signed his name to the agreement that "released the above said party from any further responsibility in the above said matter."

When the agreement had been signed, Clifter had relaxed and agreed to a cup of coffee. "I had a terrible time getting up here," he said, nibbling on a cookie. "The roads are slick as glass. Electricity is out in a lot of places. Heard there hasn't been any power along the river for three days."

Wilson thought of Frances trying to heat the cabin with firewood. It would take a lot of logs to keep the drafty old place warm. The more he thought about it, the more he worried. He decided he would have to find a way to get to her cabin and see if she were all right. But that seemed impossible. His parents had been reluctant even to let him leave his room. He didn't even dare mention Frances Crawford's name in their presence. Why did he have to feel so responsible for her? Because, if he had not met her, he would have spent the rest of his life in his own front yard working on old cars. He would have lived in the world without even seeing it.

It was after dark when Clifter left. His mother placed the dinner on the table, talking all the while. "That's the first good thing to come out of your working on the rig, Wilson. Just think how long it would have taken you to save that much money."

His father had lapsed into thought, kitchen chair tipped

back, hands folded over his stomach. "I think we could have asked for more, Wilson. I think we were a little hasty." That moment of dickering with a big company had given him a heady feeling.

But Wilson's mother disagreed. "Ty, you wouldn't want them to think we were greedy, that we were *using* Wilson's accident."

Their discussion went on all through dinner, and by the time they reached the rice pudding it was becoming heated. They hardly noticed Wilson as he left the table, saying he was a little tired and would go up to his room and rest for a while.

With his door closed behind him, he pulled on a heavy jacket and his boots, listening all the time to the rise and fall of his parents' voices downstairs in the kitchen. Lumping up a blanket, he arranged the bed to look as if he were asleep in it and turned out his light. The ice had seamed his window shut and it took all of his strength to pry it open. He stepped carefully onto the glazed roof and slid in a sitting position to the front of the house where two wooden posts held up an overhang that protected the front door. The wind blew through the neck and sleeves of his jacket and his hands were freezing from trying to get a grip on the roof's slick crust of snow. He avoided looking down. If anyone had told him a few days ago he would be climbing along the crest of a roof, he would have said they were crazy.

His ears began to ache from the wind, and the headache that had been so bad in the hospital returned. He thought of going back, but he was sure he could never crawl the distance across the roof to his room again. Lowering himself, he put his legs and arms around the pillar. It was slick, and instead of slowly shinnying down, he slid most of the way. With his feet safely on the ground, he began to shake. He realized he hadn't regained his strength, but he made himself walk toward the car.

It took only minutes to push the car down the driveway's icy incline. Once it was on the road, he was sure his parents would not hear him when he started the engine. The road was slick and Wilson could not go as fast as he wanted to, but the heater warmed him and now that he was actually on the way to Mrs.

Crawford's his headache was gone. When the road became too icy, he drove with half of the car on the sandy shoulder for traction. The farther he drove, the stronger grew his urgency to see Frances. When he reached the trail into her cabin and found the car would not climb the icy rise, he abandoned it and set out the half mile on foot.

Between the time he had left his house and arrived at Mrs. Crawford's road, the wind had changed. It blew from the south now and the ice under his feet was covered with a thin film of water. Drops of water were falling from the icicles on the trees. It was a relief not to buck the icy wind. He felt as if a spell had been broken.

The first thing he heard as he approach the cabin was the frantic barking of the dog. Wilson pushed the door open. The room was dark, the fire out, and it felt colder inside than it had outside. The dog was jumping all over him, barking and running toward the center of the room and then returning to Wilson. Wilson followed him in the dark to where Frances lay on the floor. Quickly he ran to the bedroom and, pulling the blankets off the bed, hastily wrapped them around her and lifted her onto the couch. He hurried out for logs and started up a fire. Frances looked so pale in the firelight Wilson wondered if he could manage to carry her to the car. Perhaps she ought to be in the hospital.

Frances's eyes snapped open. At first she said nothing: in dreams the cast of characters all spoke for themselves while you only watched. Then it occurred to her that it might not be a dream and she decided to test it by speaking. "Wilson, what are you doing here?" Her voice was real enough.

"I just thought I'd look in and see how you were," Wilson tried to sound casual, but he couldn't keep it up. "I think I ought to take you to the hospital."

"The hospital!" Frances sat up. "Whatever for? I'm just fine. I think I must have fallen asleep." But they both knew better.

While they talked, the light suddenly went on, like a shade going up in a darkened room to reveal the sun. "Well, better and better," she said. "I don't suppose you would know how to make a cup of tea, Wilson?" She was starting to shiver again.

He disappeared into the kitchen and she heard drawers and cupboards opening and closing. She listened to the hum of the furnace and the sound of the refrigerator. Lovely sounds, she thought. But there was an accustomed noise that was missing. The oil rig was silent. For the first time in weeks she could hear the river as it flowed noisily past the snag in front of her cabin.

When Wilson came back sloshing a tea bag up and down in a steaming mug, she asked if he could hear the well. Wilson looked for a place to put the wet tea bag, finally dropping it into an empty vase. Rather proudly he handed her the mug. "It's pretty hot." He grinned, unable to keep back the news any longer. "The rig's gone. They packed up yesterday."

She waited.

"They didn't get oil. There won't be any well there."

Frances looked at Wilson. He probably expected her to let out a cheer, to get up and dance around. But the moment was too solemn. Who could say what had guided the giant drill in its long journey down into the earth? Whatever it was, she did not believe it was chance.

The real joy, however, was not that the land was hers again and the river out of danger, but that Wilson had been restored to her.

He had more good news. "I have enough money to go to college now." He told her about Ralston Clifter's visit.

"Good for your father," she said, picturing with great satisfaction the pinched look that must have come over Ralston's face when Wilson's father asked for more money. "I just wish I had been there to cheer your dad on. But will your parents let you use it for college?"

Wilson was sure they would. "Since I had the accident, they think anything would be better than my going back to work on the rigs. All I have to do is keep on the right side of them and . . ." Wilson stumbled to an abrupt stop.

"And stay away from here," she finished for him. "I want you to know, Wilson, I don't intend to let you in my door until you're through with your first semester at school. Why should we ask for trouble? I don't blame your parents for what they feel toward me. They're absolutely right. And what about tonight? Why in heaven's name did they let you out so soon after getting home from the hospital to come over here?"

Wilson flushed.

"They don't know you're here, do they?"

She climbed out of her cocoon of blankets and pushed him toward the door. He laughed, reassured by the strength of her push.

21

The rats were a turning point.

Wilson's first weeks at college had been a disaster. Never having lived away from home before, he was uncomfortable among so many alien faces. Several times he thought he saw someone he knew from home crossing a street or walking down a hallway. But as they came closer to him, the person would turn out to be a stranger. Even the simple task of finding his way around campus on the first day of classes had defeated him. Too embarrassed to ask directions, he had been late for several of his courses. His roommate, Tim, had bought a stereo and a couple of hundred rock albums. He was expecting his drums any day. While he waited for them, Tim used his shoes or his books or tablespoons for drumming on the floor or the table or Wilson's head. He papered the walls of their room with posters of the Stones and the Beach Boys and Led Zeppelin.

While Wilson tried to study, Tim turned up the volume on the stereo and kept up a running comentary on the records: "Man, listen to those root chords. Get that chunka chunka guitar. They're running in a subtle groove, now, man. No clobbery rhythms here, man. Listen to that heavy opening." All the while punching Wilson in a friendly rhythmical way to keep his attention.

By the end of the first week of school, Tim had found a boy who played a guitar and another who played bass. They sat around in Tim and Wilson's room until two or three in the morning, jamming and practicing their reggae accents.

Worst of all were their efforts to find a name. The guitar player wanted to call the group "The Creamed Rutabagas." "Gorky," said Tim. The bass player suggested "The General Store." "Too yetch," said Tim. Tim was holding out for "The Fly Swatter."

After a couple of weeks of this, Wilson found that, in spite of himself, everything he looked at turned into a name for a rock group: The Peanut Brittle, The Wallpaper, The Shower Curtain, The Dirty Sneakers, The Stalled Engine. But it was his own suggestion that the group finally chose. They became "The Igneous Rocks." "Heavy," said Tim.

Something of Wilson's dismay must have crept into the letters to his parents, for his mother launched upon a food offensive, shipping cookies and cake nearly every day. He had written to Mrs. Crawford, too, and one morning he received a call from Professor Hogue, the head of the biology department, asking Wilson to come and see him.

Professor Hogue's office reminded Wilson of Frances Crawford's cabin. Books were piled everywhere and skins of birds and animal pelts and rocks lay on top of them. The professor was slight, with thinning white hair that stuck out in tufts over the rims of his glasses, and a way of peering intensely at you as though he were trying to remember your Latin classification.

Wilson had been nervous about the call, wondering if it was because of his poor work. With all the noise in his room he had trouble getting anything done. Still, it would be his own professor and not the head of the department who would call him in. Wilson waited while Professor Hogue replaced the point on his pencil with a jackknife, carelessly brushing the curls of wood shavings onto the floor.

"Well, sir," he said to Wilson, "I had a letter from an old

friend, Frances Crawford. Never met her, you understand, but we've gotten letters up here from her for fifty years. She's our man in the field, so to speak."

Wilson looked puzzled.

"I don't suppose you knew she was one of the first to discover the dappled warbler?"

"No, sir."

"Oh, yes, yes indeed." He took a bag of marshmallows out of his desk and offered one to Wilson, who took it out of courtesy. For a few moments they chewed silently on the flabby little pillows. "She was the first one to write us about it, nearly twenty years ago, I believe. No, more like thirty. The warbler might have been extinct now if we hadn't heard from her. We sent someone down and she tramped him around the nesting sites for days—wore him out. Oh, yes, we hear a lot from her."

It suddenly occurred to Wilson that Frances might have had something to do with his acceptance at Northern. But Professor Hogue was hurrying on between marshmallows.

"I got a letter from Mrs. Crawford yesterday." He fumbled amidst the clutter on his desk and held up a sheet of paper with Frances's familiar writing. When he put it down, it stuck to the bits of marshmallow on his hands and he had to push it onto his desk with his elbow. "She thought you might like a job."

"Yes, sir."

"How would you like to take care of the rats?"

"Rats?"

"Yes, we keep several hundred rats for our experiments. Run them through mazes and such like. Of course most of the work is done in the psychology department, but since the rats are animals and zoology is our subject, they fall under our protection, so to speak. What do you say?"

Wilson said, "Yes."

The rats were kept in a large room. Their cages, stacked from floor to ceiling, covered all four walls. Each time you entered the room, hundreds of white shapes skittered back and forth and hundreds of pink eyes stared. The room smelled of disinfectant and the pellets of grain that were fed to the rats. It was Wilson's job to come in once a day, feed the animals, and fill their water bottles. On Saturdays he cleaned the cages, carefully removing the rats by their tails. Occasionally one developed a middle-ear disease, and when he picked it up by its tail, it twirled around like a mechanical toy and had to be disposed of. Often there would be babies in the cages, their pink hairless bodies and pug faces looking more like miniature pigs than rats. His new job gave Wilson a place to study at night; his grades, which had been unspectacular, began to improve.

And there was Melissa, who shared the job with him. At first they had come at different times. Then, finding they enjoyed each other's company, they worked together. On Saturdays when they cleaned the cages, Melissa arrived in grubby jeans with her waist-length red hair done up in a scarf and went at the cages like a pile of dirty dishes. She was going to be a veterinarian and was fascinated by the rats, fussing over the sick ones and counting the number of new babies each week.

Evenings they sat together in the lab doing their homework —pink rats' eyes watching their every move, soft, throaty squeaks of encouragement issuing out of cages.

Like Wilson, Melissa had been raised in the country and loved the outdoors. They rented cross-country skis, and when they finished on Saturdays, headed for the gently rolling hills that ringed the small college town, following deer and raccoon tracks and stopping under the shelter of pine trees to watch the thick flakes of snow fall around them.

One day, Wilson thought, Melissa would come and visit him in Oclair and he would take her to Frances Crawford's. He knew they would get along. He didn't care if his parents approved of Melissa; it was Frances's opinion that counted. He wanted to take Melissa there because he always brought Frances the rare things he found.

22

Day after day the melting snow and ice from the roof dripped down until a narrow trough formed like a miniature moat around Frances's cabin. Snow disappeared from the bases of the trees, leaving rings of exposed ground. A gray meadow vole tunneled out and sat blinking in the sun. Brown paper packets of seed arrived in the mail.

Frances ticked off the order of returning birds: red-winged blackbird, phoebe, robin, wood duck, cowbird, mourning dove, kingfisher, swallow, white-throated sparrow, grackle, and then a yellow explosion of spring warblers.

Plants pushed up through the earth. Much of the first foliage emerging from the ground was red, as if the leaves were bruised and bloody from their struggle with stones and cold ground. She knew better of course; it was simply the presence of anthocyanin pigments in the plants without the masking effect of chlorophyll. So much for her romantic speculations.

Warm days came, but they were followed by cold, rainy days with nights that dipped down into the twenties, too cold to set out the vegetables she had started indoors. Her seedlings wavered tremulously in coffee cans and milk cartons. They were a pale green, and too leggy.

Although she had received only two letters from Wilson, she thought of him often, pleased that his second letter had been so much more enthusiastic than the first one. When she had gone to college, only a few women took science courses and she was not one of them. She took a vicarious pleasure in Wilson's description of his work. Professor Hogue had written her that after a shaky beginning Wilson was one of the best students. For some reason she couldn't understand, Hogue's letters were always sticky, the pages adhering stubbornly to one another and to her fingers. Perhaps it was some paste he used in his research?

Each morning when she went down to see the river, Frances looked over at the clearing where the well had been, but she had not been able to make herself walk over and inspect it. She thought of it as a battlefield and half expected to look over one day and see a monument looming over the empty acres.

Wilson came to see her at the end of June. The dog exploded into a frenzy of recognition, prancing and bucking and springing up to lick Wilson's face. Frances and Wilson were shy with each other. Wilson no longer looked like a boy. He had grown a shaggy blond beard; since his blue eyes were about all you could see of him now, they appeared larger and more arresting. Frances thought there might be things he could tell her that she did not know.

Wilson found Frances more fragile. The fine cross-hatch of lines on her face had deepened, and when she walked into the kitchen to fetch him some raspberry juice, she walked with less assurance.

"How is school, Wilson?" Frances asked rather formally when she returned with the juice.

"Well, it's funny. You learn a lot of technical stuff, the kind of things you have to memorize, like the parts of plants and their Latin names. But I think I learned a lot more just walking through the woods with you." It was painfully embarrassing to Wilson to bring this out, but it was true and, seeing how frail Frances was, he was determined to tell her.

Frances was pleased. "I'm not sure but what you're right, Wilson. It was the great naturalists who tramped through the countryside and kept their eyes open, men like Thoreau and Muir and Burroughs, who taught us the most about nature."

Wilson began to feel more at home. No one had quoted at him for a long time. "I've got a friend, a girl friend, I'd like to have you meet some time. When she comes to visit me, I'll bring her over."

Frances smiled. Secretly she had sometimes thought Wilson was ashamed of their friendship, that he would be afraid his friends would think she was old and strange and the cabin slovenly.

Wilson had brought his fishing gear and together they walked toward the river. It was still high from the spring run-off and had a rushed, exuberant sound. The river had its own special smell that was like nothing else. It was a musty odor of wet grasses and pine and the slightly bitter smell of bracken. It made Wilson anxious to get into his waders and slip into the stream, but his eyes kept returning to the clearing. He hesitated. Frances followed the direction of his glance, recalling the white ghostly shape of the derrick that had appeared in her dream. Wilson thought of his last night on the rig, of the block dropping toward the ground. He knew he would never get over what had happened unless he could bring himself to return to the site and stare his demon down.

Reluctantly, Frances followed him. The oil company had plowed over the clearing and sown grass in the furrows. Deer had come to graze on the tender new shoots; their tracks were everywhere. Wilson and Frances found several patches of clover on the site, a few sorrel plants, plantain, and a creeping cinquefoil. Wilson spotted some woolly mullein leaves, and Frances found a wild strawberry plant.

By the end of the summer their list had grown to include bracken, wild honeysuckle, blackberries, two species of violets, dandelions, ragweed, pearly everlastings, and a choke-cherry seedling.

The following spring, when Wilson brought Melissa to meet

Frances, the three of them discovered a three-foot-high poplar, wild raspberries, eight kinds of grasses and spurge. The trees that had stood marshaled into rows at the edge of the clearing had begun to march; oak and maple seedlings were coming up. The birds had spread Juneberries from the bushes along the riverbank. On the side of the clearing nearest the river, they discovered two spikes of wide-leaved ladies'-tresses. The blooms of the tiny wild orchid were no larger than a half-inch across. They were a buff color, with a lip of pale yellow threaded with delicate green lines.

In all her years of looking, Frances had never before found the plant on her property. She decided there was no end to the miracles the land could produce.